A Quincy History

James Haining

A LUCKY HEART BOOK

Salt Lick Press • *Quincy, Illinois*
1981

Some poems in this volume were previously published in the Salt Lick Sampler *A Quincy History,* © 1975 by Salt Lick Press. Grateful acknowledgment to the editors of anthologies in which work in this volume has appeared, viz: *Spatial Poem,* ed. Mieko Shiomi (1976, Osaka); *Way of Art,* ed. Odair Magalhaẽs, Vivenciàl Activity Studio (1975, São Paulo); *Beowulf to Beatles: the varieties of poetry,* ed. David Pichaske (Macmillan, 1981).

Grateful acknowledgment is also made to the editors of the following magazines in which some verse in this book first appeared: *Southwest Review, The New Journal, december, The Shore Review, Granite, Sumac, Asphalt, Stinktree, Happiness Holding Tank, The Chicago Review, Some, Twigs, X: a Journal of the Arts, Amaranthus, The Living Wilderness, The Spoonriver Quarterly,* and *Salt Lick.*

"Kitchen Talking" was published in the Poetry On The Buses Program by the Illinois Arts Council, 1979, funded in part by the National Endowment for the Arts.

First edition. A Lucky Heart Book. Copyright © 1981 by Salt Lick Press, Inc. Post Office Box 1064/Quincy, Illinois 62301   All rights reserved.

Printed in the United States of America.

This book was partially funded by a grant from the Illinois Arts Council.

A Quincy History is the eleventh Lucky Heart Book to be published by Salt Lick Press.

No part of this book may be reproduced by any means, nor translated into a machine language without the written permission of the publisher.

This book was designed and set at National ShareGraphics, inc. for Lucky Heart Books.

NOTE: stanza breaks at the bottom of a page
are signaled by asterisks in the footline.

Library of Congress Cataloging in Publication Data:

Haining, James, 1950–

    A Quincy History.
    A Lucky Heart Book.

    I.   Title.
PS3558.A33205   811'.54   81–2049
ISBN 0–913198–02–1   AACR2

10 9 8 7 6 5 4 3 2 1

For
Christine & Ridge

For
my family

A QUINCY HISTORY

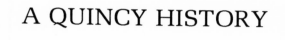

1-15-72

It strikes me that maybe I should be listing rules of some sort on this the first page of my first journal, but I'm a bit lost tonight. Picked up Lally's journal and found some there, but put the book down when I realized what it was; felt like I had been in somebody's field when I shouldn't have. So, so. Verse coming in a whimper these days; got to collect the scraps flying round the desk. No entries in the ms. since the end of the *Circle.* So much going on makes the self-perspective of his impossible.

I have decided over the balance of the stay in Quincy that I should make my first book ms. *very soon.* Planning on *Ramblin Rose + The Circle +* 20 poems all written prior to the completion of *Circle;* this 45 poem ms. leaves me several choices on what to try: *RR + Circle* for a chap to be called *25 Poems* (Burns's idea); maybe a small chap of the 20 loose poems to gain some leverage. I would like the ms. at any rate to come out from a large house, if at all possible. If I were 30 (having done nothing more than I already have), I would be held in higher esteem by the general publishing world. But, I'm not.

1-18-72/11:30 P.M.

Worked on the magazine all day since the folios arrived from Dan and the flyers were done too; so finally getting some of them on the road.

Almost finished typing up the ms. completely last night. A few still loose, but under a weight on the desk. Some of them felt good from the start and were one shots like "The Wrench" and "Kitchen Talking." Some nice things happening in others almost. There is something wrong with "Seeing," and I can't see just what it is yet. Maybe the ending which was runover when typing it. Stringing the beads in the middle was the hard part, but I guess I forgot to look up when the ending went by. Will have to live with the poem for a while.

Since doing *Circle,* the events occurring about me probably have been making great excuses for not doing any work; but going back, I usually find that I've done more work than I thought at first. Nothing quite that new about that or many of the other things which are constantly amazing me, but it is a discovery for me.

New issue of *december* with my poem and a story by Lally. Later on the phone Lally says that he would make a great hack writer (". . . really!) as he is surprised at the quality of the story upon reading for the first time since done in '69. He also highly praises my poem. It's the first time he has seen it on the page (he had heard it before) and he couldn't explain it. Good hope. Burns is the only one who usually looks close enough to see what the belly of the poem is like. And I do believe that the subtle mechanics of some of my verse is probably the best work I have done. And no one looks. Burns and Lally maybe now. Shit. This is ridiculous.

1-21-72/11:30 P.M.

Just leafed through the new book by Joe Bruchac and *S403* by David McAleavey. *S403* seems to be another book out from Ithaca House because he is at Cornell. That's all I can see. Bruchac's book is half/half. His directions in African lit as well as American Indian lit/scenery make me question his motives. The poems that deal with these two areas seem to be inferior to the others. He is more at home when using his own biographical material in building the poem; examples of this are "Cochise," "For My Sister In S.F.," and "For My Grandfather in Greenfield Center."

Also saw two really bad cycle films at the CRESCENT tonight.

Rejections from *The Paris Review* and *The Red Cedar Review* today and a dream: everything concerning the dream has been repressed. Must have been great since the only part I remember is that I wanted to remember it, so I could do a poem from it. New kitten next door.

1-25-72

Wrecked again!! But much good work done today which makes my head lighter. Mailed out ⅔ of the mag and received a nice letter from a man named Martinblum from Milwaukee who was impressed with the issue. Called the work "important." Good for him. Says he's to do a review of littles, and we will be there.

So much trouble with making the ms. (making it from what is already here/making it harder), because I choose a 45 poem package (*Ramblin Rose* + *Circle* + 20) and the 20 is hard. I don't feel like I have that many worth it. For this reason, I may keep the end of the ms. open so that I can pull out weaker poems for better ones as they are written. Trouble with that is that the new ones will seem better because of the proximity. Already said this. At this point, I'll keep the size instead of cutting it down. I don't think, I don't want, the particular poem that as it stands against another, falls not as tall (not short) is thrown out; its simple self should fill. The hole in the ms. that would exist without it.

That's why it's hard I suppose.

Sent Gerald Burns a ms. of the newer poems today. First ms. to him in a while I think. Since *Circle.* "Seeing For" (minus the last stanza), "Kitchen Talking," "The Wrench," "The Roads," and "Model" (which is old, but I don't think he ever saw it).

Maybe a small run of poems or a longer poem in these poems that began as *Things For Ralph.* Sort of reminds me of *Jensen—A Slide Show,* and I don't want that either way. Four so far: "For Ralph," "Seeing" for, "Calico" for, and "Rules" for. Have to get some ms. out tomorrow.

1-26-72

Sitting before the first real fire in our fireplace (Dan had a small one of building scraps when I was in New York in November.)

Also bought two Creeley works today: *The Charm* and *A Quick Graph.* The first poem that Creeley published is so nice/smooth as silk. All the gossip about him now—even from Hollo—is a bummer. Hope to get a better view from the essays. I always liked his fiction best to now.

1-27-72

"Out yonder there was this huge world, which exists independently of us human beings and which stands before us like a great eternal riddle, at least partially accessible by inspection and thinking." —A. Einstein (I. D. *The Beginnings of Albert Einstein*)

The poems which exist without us are the only true poems. Those which are not of these (flooding the littles now; as always—totally in the head, totally conceived with no revisions, and of course high quality) are more to be valued as technical achievements. From my limited knowledge, this accounts for the NY mob except for O'Hara. Owing

Gerald for setting me *quite* straight on this point with found-poems, exercises. And actually the best exercise for each of us is the one we can create for ourselves, built to strengthen that which is weakest about us, no secret to each. Many of my weaker poems are exercises/half completions of whatever end in alignment. "The Watched Bird" and "Sundance" done almost the same sitting: TWB first as the trying on; when I could see and feel the poem (head) better, finally making "Sundance" in the conclusion.

Ms. today to Larcomb and T. Johnson. Both requested. The magazine at U. of Miami of Ohio will reprint half of *Ramblin Rose* and give me $8.00. Fine with me. Also a story of sorts.

I don't know if I've found any of the natural poems or not. I don't think conception of a verse in an instant before striking to paper automatically makes for a rock or tree poem. Maybe "Message To The Chief" is a natural. Maybe simply well trained, nocturnal poet doing what the elves did for the shoemaker (if Castelaz could only hear me now.)

1-27-72/1:30 AM

THOSE FAVORITE

—After Robert Creeley

    things that wear
    so well the years
    they are around
    coffee cup   paring knife
    until the morning
    they stop   leaving
    quietly the way
    they came

Tonight in class (doing Olson), I began to wonder if he would recognize a tree as a considerable poem. A construct to be sure of energy composed with true regard to that which coexists (wind, water, land, sun, man, etc.)

Doing WCW next week and looking forward to that. Going to buy his essays and maybe an earlier collection. Then read all I can trying to absorb him. The class this week was good, but I expect the WCW class to be *real fine.*

1-28-72/2 AM

Back from D.C. tonight where Dan, Michael, Tina and I listened to Irwin Silber w/ Barbara Dane for some 2½ hours at the Community Book Store. A few good points in what was mostly a long evening on a long bench.

Lots of mail with interesting surprises including a rare letter from DiPalma. Rare in that all he said was that he was happy to be in the issue and to please send a copy to his mother . . . letter from Bruchac with high praise for this one and telling me that he likes to publish in the magazine, also sending a ms. he said . . . flyers from Larcomb for *Asphalt 4,* and he dug the issue. A day that was really nice to begin with so much good feeling. Also realized that finding uncanceled stamps on letters received is a good luck sign: I got 12¢ of postage that way today. And Burns. He put together a ms. along the lines of the tentative one I sent him from my letters and correspondence. Very happy about it with some reservations about some of the really early things ("Sea Poem," "Southwest," etc.) with better things later as their substitution. He also said some interesting things about my newer work: the fact that he could see himself in them rather than David who in some ways I see there. Also: ". . . save the coming tougher, sinewy new ones (at least those you haven't written yet) for a new book to match what I take to be the new sound, the secret being that it's like a *sound*-bloc that makes a 'sequence,' & certainly a book, not subject or such. It's a way of seeing that all the poems saying the same things (since their sound is what they say) are together."

And it is so. The language music being scored dense or sparsely in lines. Breaks being so important to me, although at times it must look like a silly game. Mostly if light, I enjoy it for myself and hope that no one else bothers with it. And I guess they don't. But Burns sees it, even if he doesn't acknowledge it all the time. He's right on sequence, it seems. *Ramblin Rose* being a pulling of the earliest poems worth saving and doing a new one or so once I felt it again to go with them. *Circle* was closer to the letter in definition since I was half way through the poems that made it before I really caught the sound/shape/music (I wish there was a word for it); then the balance of the poems came in support of what I already knew and poem that simply happened then. The last poem being the result of a discussion with McDonell on rejecting the myth of the straight line. Talking with him about that which exists between two positions, the straight line being the tool given us to understand space, distance. A circle seemed to be a logical substitution, having added dimensions to encompass the folds and turns in our lives. Possibly a mite pretentious, but right. Will probably drop the short preface that went with the first two copies w/

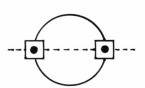 illustration explaining poems in the cycle as being different places on the circle. One point being birth, the later being death. I suppose the distance between some are much less than others. Actually. One point is both life and death with the other point being the mark of consciousness (all experience to this point being of a sensory data nature). The size of the circle being determined by duration of life rather than intellect; the poems in *Circle* run a far range from The Mailman's Dilemma to Text; all places to live through.

1-30-72

The name for this first collection or one to come is *Rob-*

ert E. Lee. Not that a single poem or reference in notes, letters, etc. floated before this time; I thought about him many times in half-regard to him because of supposed blood ties and character reconstructions. Robert E. Lee means more about the generations than the man personally. Just as my poetry in the collection, by whatever name, is more a discussion of that around me. Sympathies about the south from the romantic escaping fantasy that kept me alive as a child in hard conflict with consciousness/which is real—seeing as all the faults in the earth closed one by one by one. May do something with this/might not use it/will continue to think about it.

1-31-72

The Magician's Apprentice

who would hold
the hat the
wand when it
was late
and the time
was for bed

sweeping the floor
until it was
quiet   quiet night

The mention of *REL* as a title to Lee Lally met with favorable response. Michael didn't know yet. I don't know. Got to sleep very soon.

2-2-72

A few letters of interest in last days, including the always unexpectable expectable letter from Gerald. His reactions to the magazine, but this time he was so excited that he didn't really pick at the lint in it. I suppose that will come later on in NYC. Haven't heard from Bob & Ginger as yet, but they were pleased is the impression from Gerald's letter. Maybe he is right, and this issue is built on many of the old beams and joints of *Origin.* If so, Olson would probably enjoy this number/s.*

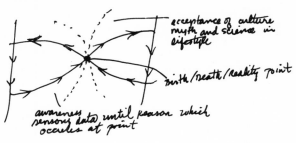

The Chance

is making
our music
the way
we do now

in the room
which is
crimson the
house justice
city living

As the key I use for understanding this sound. My first book. So it will become one of the 20 poems sandwiched in between *Ramblin Rose* and *Circle* while it was written after *Circle,* as well as "Wrench" and "Kitchen Taking"; they, well one, resembles the same as in *Circle,* although the other

*A double issue of [the magazine] *Salt Lick,* including Robert Trammell's *Famous Men* as a separable chapbook.

is an oddball in *Circle,* the chance. This poem as a footnote. Oh no. That sounds like too many of the people who I criticize.

The right combinations of sound and the right rhythm music. I suppose this started with the tranquility on "Text." Thinking of Creeley with the title. Easy.

After thinking of a poem written some time in the past, exact moment unclear, it showed up on the back of a scrap of paper in Diane Nextdoorneighbor's medical notebook. Seems I was over for the night when Dan was ill. Done over at her place way back in October or November.

> *Western*
>
> it was the
> indian shot
>
> camera
> low angle to
> the ground
> our indians
> line
> across the crest
> of the hill
> black string
> of beads

The object to make the third section of the book as strong as the cycles. Trimming a few seems necessary. Those for sure:

1. Everyone's River Poem
2. Starting Back Toward The Cabin
3. Poem For Father Going Crosscountry
4. The Chance

2-6-72

Sound as legislator of the poem. Sound as punctuation. Reading an old letter from Burns where he had been irritated from the lack of uniform capitalization and uneven punctuation. Eric used to bitch on this point as well. So: the word/sound at the end of the line directing the traffic. Correct breathing for *MY* lungs. Ginsberg talking about how he learned breath. Then *Wichita Vortex Sutra* . . .

2-7-72/5:00 PM

Tool

holding the awl
the scan of the
field   your hands
the way to
roll with your
children mother

standing in
the door or on
a flat run

> it would take
> all of these
>
> to be the crafts
> man   a dish

A bad poem but a good point. Started in a letter to Wm. Hart today. Craft for the poet is taught more through his feet and hands than reading anyone, or talking a good game with his teammates. Once thought about organizing a team of sorts for Salt Lick complete with team shirts with patch on the back for easy recognition and name on the shoulder. Most magazines these days would do better to recognize their clubbyness early and organize. Again, nature as master. Dealing with all through this. For me this is where Emerson/Whitman come in; just that in America these days, we are conceited enough to think that the poem is dropped into our head by God or antichrist for the professed godless, and we're off to the races etc. When will this America. God's promised land end. Probably hold here and move on.

2-8-72

Completed *Robert E. Lee* late tonight. Feel basically good about it. *Circle* still a bit uneasy. Holding at 15 poems. Same as the list with "Abortion" being the exception. Sending GB a copy and showing one to Michael as well—the idea being to see if I have blind spots they can catch.

Phone to GB, sounds receptive to *Lee*. Have to get it done soon so I can move on. So hard going through those odd bits and trying to find a line for them. Nice to find things in some of them I had no knowledge of. Sound starting to do itself, but no poem itself being a step. And as best I can recall subject or image being the drive. I have a better feel for *Circle* after going through the mistakes before it. But then Poem For Father surprises me, at the line/breaks when it was pure emotion in the writing. ⅔ literal from our conversation. Seven of the fifteen poems of the section not appearing in print elsewhere which cuts down on the credits in the front. Don't know if the book will impress anyone (houses) or not as is, but doing the *Circle* in the next issue of the magazine. Also might interest a local concern.

2-11-72

Barbara

the four doors of
our apartment we
say we live in
while going through
one means leaving
the other room or
closet   smaller rooms
where our clothes
stay
      everytime I open
      a door the room
      changes

Such beautiful Creeley tonight. Although *The Charm* is easily seen as early works that entertain, but so uneven. I wonder if *Lee* is that same. Typing up some of the older poems for *Circle* was sad in some way due to their for the most being stale. Fun finding overlooked plus things. Glad that I am working to keep me straight while pulling the ms. together . . . it escapes me how people can make previously published poems the scale of value while making the book ms. Don't say that they trust the editor's judgment; any other time, editors to the poet seem to be the men grading papers. This coming from the fact that my tendency at this point is to overlook these poems in favor of poems that seem stronger in the ms. *Ramblin Rose* the exception because the poems were poems *I chose* to have published, not Drake. He chose to print them, but trusted me. They will be out soon, so I can see what the intro is like. Sort of got me worried, but Bud says it is justifiable—any claims immediately made are borne out in the cycle.

2-21-72

And so.

Mr. Roberts

it's the story of water
seeing the whole convoy
running by night

silhouettes

Mr. Roberts is dead   along
with another officer drinking
coffee   by the Zero

Frank, do you hear me?

Mr. Roberts

Frank, do you hear me?
it's the story of water

drinking coffee with another
officer in a forward room
he died with the Zero

Mr. Roberts is dead

it's the story of water
seeing the whole convoy
running by night   flat tops
sweepers and big cans
silhouettes for the new
generation

2-28-72

The problem is that *Lee* is done, and I can feel it. Getting the book published is not the last step in completing it (the problem with so many I think); but because I feel it done and unpublished, hustling it is dreadful business. Even Burns thinks of it as being in print. And if I simply continue with the new work, I could fall into the predicament that Lally and Burns find themselves in; Burns because of the next step and Michael because of *everything.* Joyce Varney knows some people in a half-dozen houses. So, I guess I will let her send it around for a year or so till it finds a home. Still thinking to put *Circle* in this next issue. Will try not to think about the issue for the next month though and let it ride.

3-4-72

The Bomber

among the crowd
on the corner   he
waits   the restaurant
across the way

he is the kitchen
helper or either a
busboy since

both were unaccounted
for that day

the one much bigger
dark   than the
other but the short
man the least likely
to be noticed

he must have known
that it would
be crowded

Near Liberty, Illinois

it is a trail, now
a path because the first
walk became daily.

The thing that would
be there knowing
the ways trees look when
dry and wet, how to
dress.

Start into the wash,
follow the stream to
the fence and walk
fence for a half mile,
then the same across,
then up again.

We had a square,
a hundred-sixty acres,
half mile half mile.

A day is four times this.

3-5-72

Journey

It is along the same
road that first took
you there that you go
now.

The way it happens
as it did knowing
the times between
light   to   sign   to
building   and get away.

But this time through
is the first only again
having to see   the place
where there was to be this
crime.

Hard time to title this one. Clumsy at best I'm sorry to
say.

Whitney

puma on the
sandstone ledge
where he killed
rabbit two days
before

Met Ray Johnson at his 3/4/72 opening at Jacobs Gallery in D.C. after getting a strange special delivery letter asking me to "get my ass" down for it. Another crazy. Guess he has been around. He saw my piece in the show in Chicago along with the *Salt Lick.* So, he says he *will* be in touch.

These newer poems somewhat handicapped because I have not shifted my gears yet. Trying to do some longer pieces. Have not been able to do a whole poem in my head any longer in length. Not able to do it and then remember. Also has something there beyond the immediate flash. Won't go as Frost and say that the ending is as surprise to me (just sometimes), but I have to look in a new way. A bit harder, not especially closer, but long enough to blur the first object seen and then see the atmosphere standing around it. Like relatives you see in the family photos after looking at yourself, first.

3-10-72

Two

there was another girl
twin to Lucile who
lived only three years

not so poor as lean
the family buried the
baby halfdimes the year
she was born to cover
her eyes

always coins
the right years
from anyones

pocket there beside
the grave the coins
the right years not so
hard to find for our
children on their last day

Of course I wanted to say more, but couldn't very well because of the way the idea came clean on that single connection. A floater. Sent GB poems today for the first time in a while. Ones out of the journal. After typing up, "Bomber," "Barbara," and "Those Favorite." Still dragging ass w/ *Lee,* wrecked again.

I Want To Talk To You

because of the new paint
the house isn't the same
there seems to be more
because all the rooms are
white

since I'm really tired
of hearing myself here

with the new language
I've got not afraid of
her listening

3-16-72

On the train now for NYC and a visit. Driving Dan Mc-Donell to the airport to catch his ride to Chicago, it occurred to me that I might make a list of the music I have been listening to lately for future reference:

McLaughlin	Hendrix
Miles	Allman Bros.
Coryell	Rundgren
Jack Bruce	Johnny Winter
Roy Buchanan	Tull
Taj Mahal	The Band
Zappa	Santana
John Hammond	Savoy Brown
Steve Miller	B.B. King
Tony Williams	Fleetwood Mac
Spirit	Edgar Winter
Who	Crazy Horse
J. Airplane	Leslie West
Led Zepplin	Leon
Little Feat	Climax Blues Band
J. Giles	Judy Collins
Grin	Humble Pie
McCartney/Lennon	CSNY
Marc Benno	Harrison
Loggins & Messina	Poco
John Baldry	Clapton/D&D

Met John Cage today when he appeared at Maryland Art Institute and read for an hour or so from his journal. Interesting that he mentioned Geo. Leonard besides Fuller and Mao. Lots of Mao and Fuller, equating some sort of cake and eat it too. He gave me his address and we talked a bit about the work Ray Johnson has been doing. He seemed *very* tired, but cheered up when a girl gave him a bag of mushrooms.

3-24-72

On way to NYC again. On train just out of Baltimore; in a tunnel in fact. I hope this is readable after writing it. The train speed.

There is a beautiful girl across the aisle. She is wearing a soft brown shirt that is the same color as her hair. Her eyes must be brown too. She is reading. The idea just occurs that trains are wonderful (Gerald/David's word) because in a car, excepting one with a bar or diner, people stay in a place. They will leave and come back again sometimes, but it is their seat. They keep their luggage there because it is their seat, or it is their seat because their luggage is there. On a just

(over water)

over short trip people who use the stool will use it more than once; people will wait until off the train to use a stool.

There are two college girls behind me (U of Baltimore on a notebook) talking. They will stop just before getting off.

An ensign across and up the aisle reading that new Hemingway novel (the one first in Esquire). I saw a stand of those in a grocery store.

Two people walk by.

A man less than crisp (ensign) in green corduroy, balding, can't stop looking out the smokey window. The girl with brown looks out the window, holding her book.

Reference

the old pilings
from the bridge
since torn down
are even in
their row

brown a foot
and so above
the waterline

some weeds from
the wind or birds

the bridge in
Quincy isn't like
this much bigger
it straddles a
channel

when they were
building that one
the divers who
did the first
work   watching the
bottom setting forms

they said that
they had seen
catfish down there
bigger than them

by the time the
stories had been through
the bars they had
asked for more money
and they got it

5-4-72

So many strange things happening around me. Some
inside. Last night in D.C. with Dan, Michael, and Lee to hear
Ed Cox read with Wendy Apt and Reed Whittemore.
Whittemore and Apt both bad and leave it at that. Ed with
such energy. I left the room smiling. Afterward, went to the
Cairo, old rundown hotel once hangout for F. Scott Fitzger-
ald. Great place with all drinks 50¢, but only straight or with

soda or water. We were there with several from the reading. Many gay friends of Michael. He has been through so many changes, but he never is complacent about a direction since as soon as he knows he is headed one way he puts his energy to it. He speaks of his gay consciousness as the most liberating event of his life. We are able to do some honest talking for a change. I was amazed to hear some of the new things he felt he had learned, not so much because of my now knowing the event, but because I didn't know him. And so many of the problems he has finally seen through were never my problems. Lee says that I'm the only straight that she has ever been able to talk to.

I don't know if I can accept Michael's idea that a heterosexual relationship is built on sexism. He tells me not to look at the implications or I'll blow my circuits which I believe since what I know now is very trying. But the ENERGY that comes from dealing/trying to touch these problems is tremendous. Rita May Brown, D.C. radical lesbian poet, says that when you are weakest, you are stronger. Carry that out. Each time you can stand with successive layers of defense, myth, etc. stripped down leaving nothing between yourself and truth, you do get stronger. Sometimes that strength allows suicide. The closer you get to truth, the more it exacts from you. The more you are of it.

The last weekend in NYC to see David was very disappointing. Maybe mostly my fault, but from what Ginger and Felicia have said, I know there were other things going on. David is a genius; we all know that. Sometimes I used to think that the thing that differs us was his family background being financially stable. Thus, he was indulged. I was tolerated. But I found that out of his domain, he was hard pressed to simply get along in a group—obsessed with being the center of attention which led to some rather dismal times spent in various bars and at Bob & Ginger's. The four of us were never together: me-David-Bob-Gerald, and I suppose there was nothing that said we should have been. That was me dreaming. So I learned a bit through that.

David and I did talk for a while Saturday afternoon about verse. Seems we come from different corners toward the poem. He says, ". . . you base the poem in experience or reality where I don't." I suppose that's true enough. By basing his poem in the hypothetical, or theory, he has control. David can't seem to function in an uncontrolled situation. But he says nice things about my verse which I find hard to believe sincere. Maybe this is my problem, not his.

4-6-72

Home

each time they fall
from around me
seeing now as I am
before it
      there is more
each time I have moved
knowing where it is
is last   energy a
better form of us

3-28-72 For Michael Lally

Going to NYC tomorrow night. Dan McD going with me this time. Tickets for a Sunday night concert and backstage party. Excited at the prospects. Good bit of luck. Got a card from Grover Lewis at *Rolling Stone* who enjoyed the magazine and said he would see what he could do about a review. First response to a large batch of review copies I sent out lately. Hope to get a chance to visit with Gerald. I understand that David's contact at Lippincott is very promising. Good. Hope that is the kick in the ass he needs to get some new work done.

4-11-72
Huntington, W. Va.

We pull into town in the rain at 5 a.m. this morning after a long night drive through the Appalachian Mountains. Marshall University. Due for a 3:00 p.m. reading in just a few hours and then again at 7 this evening. We both pull $75.

Intro For Michael

1.   Voice.

2.   History which is not only a way
      of knowing things, but personally
      a way of seeing. Great journalism.

3.   Let's call the way you walk, think,
      and write politics. Also love. Or
      let's call nothing political.

4.   Think about using a word as well as
      the idea so it is the word. Great
      poetry does this.

4-14-72

Home now for a few days and still rather undone. Tired. Both readings good. The evening one especially and Michael surprising me with his intro for me. He was very moving. Also he called today to say that he just won the Discovery Contest put on by the YMHA in NYC. He gets a

small sum of money but a very large amount of publicity.
Very happy for him.

Ginger

earth mother does not live
in you   if she does not live
in me   each of us   host

which means I don't expect
you to make breakfast
I used to but not now

when I visit you keep
saying I'm not there
but I am what there
is to visit   maybe
stays at the house

4-18-72

Much done today. House work. Floors. And the desk.
Caught up on letters too. Recorded work for Al Austin's
Black Box the other day. Not so hot. The thing with Ginger
still unsettling me. Bruce Andrews and Nathan Whiting also
there. Nathan distant, grubby, and after all loveable. Bruce
with a mind like a house afire. Great conversation that
night. I'm surprised that he even listens to my work due to
where he is writing these days. But we talked. Felt each
other out. A curious energy in his verse. I don't see much
more than that now, but he is still going. At his stage, he is
personally out of the poetic, but when he moves in, hummm.
I mean I can only listen to so much theory. Very fast mind.

Blue Is Green—Miles Davis
John McLaughlin

Meeting Mahavishnu was very quiet. Felissa there absorbing the moment. Such a quiet man who dances with his guitar. I could feel the energy in his presence. The concert is the best I've ever seen for sure. Such control. 2600 people quiet when he spoke.

4-22-72

Calico For Gladine

flour in fifty pound
sack sugar in twenty
pound sacks   theres
still some this way

print muslin making
the sacks not seem
to be what they are
holding things but

these sacks make
into dresses shirts
aprons the only
trouble is that
no two sacks
are the same never
enough of one
color except for
baby

4-26-72

Weak, tired, and trying to rest today. I believe it is against my nature to rest. Suppose my mother could tell me different though. Stomach trouble. Canceling most all activities until Saturday.

Artists occur at points on the line which is history. No artist lived before his time. His work is at best timely. The greatest artist being the joiner. Synthesis. The ones who take civilization with them. Not so much what is led, but can be followed.

5-11-72

The temptation is to protect the artist for those who comprehend his position (but not his work necessarily). There is no best way to protect him or to be protected *from* him. It is a curious love that goes on here. This is starting to sound like a dust-jacket blurb which is probably the first clue to stop. Honestly, these things seem to be clear at this time to me.

Two days back from a *very* rushed trip to Quincy. No time to pack. Fly to St. Louis and Randy & Betty there to catch me. Home by midnight. No Barbara, so I went to bed. An hour later Barbara finds me. She had been out tripping. Very shaken by my being there; happy though. We were happy to be together, but avoided discussion about the problems. This could be that nothing will come of the relationship other than being lovers. Maybe that is enough.

So, back to Balto with terrible flying connections. Was with Dan for half an hour between flights in Chicago. Good to see him. A bit troubled to hear of his school/hour troubles. Wish I had the money to lay on him. He wants to go back to Italy which strikes me as a good idea. I decided over the balance of my stay in Quincy to move back when I can, probably the middle of June. The energy I'm losing here from the situation is hurting my output. No headway on my health either. Picked up a throat infection they are trying to tell me may be mono. I don't think it is, but blood test knows for sure tomorrow. I do know this: I have never wanted to be healthier in my life.

> *Revival*
>
> again
>
> our having to
> always talk about
> home   the house
>
> when we mean
> survival we say
> self-preservation
> not later or the
> next one

> because I'm quiet
> quiet   because
> I'm quietly
> the size I
> am new
> friends see
> me wrong
> at   first
> sometimes

5-12-72

Doctors tell me as of the morning that I have infectious mono. Quite a blow. I wasn't really ready to hear that. The day spent in catching up on mail and trying to make some sense of what I should do. Looks as if I may be moving within the week. This is such a bad time. Looks like I will have to cancel my class, the 23rd reading. I am very tired.

Vita

quiet
because I'm quietly the
size I am people
expect me to make
more noise than I do
moving through the room
is only your idea
of me being somewhere else

5-14-72

Must shake this depression that is lying on me. Just the prospects of all that is before me. Randy will be here in five days to drive me back. Talked some with Dan tonight about why this is closing this way. Had to make him see it as clearly as I could. *Rolling Stone* article came today making for irony. Finally so unimportant. Perhaps it is the anticipation of starting. I wish it was tomorrow that I were climbing in the car for the drive. Not knowing what there is for me back in Illinois. Only myself which it is time to meet again. I don't know if Barbara will be there. I surely can't expect her. As it is, I'm pushing people away from me now.

Baltimore

now that   I can
talk about it the
problems I have
been having with

my health I mean
holding it past
something I've been
thinking I have to
now lay down this
the second time
I've been to the
mountain   time
there its getting
back which isn't
just right

5-27-72

First entry since back in Illinois. Have been back a full
week now, but not so much to show for it. Got a post office
box and made the usual changes there so the mail will be
flowing again. All my things still packed and currently sitting here with me in Chris's basement. Blood and urine tak-
en for tests Wednesday when I see Borden. Then, I can begin to get settled. Even if it means not unpacking all my stuff
for another month (it's hard not to work if all the tools are
lying around.)

Don't know as yet about Barbara. Good to be together,
but that is as lovers. We usually avoid talking. The only way
I can be for now is simply not to expect anything from her.
That way I won't imagine things, and she has the freedom
she must have. Sounds silly when on the page here, but it is
this way.

Finishing the *december* feature very soon now. I have a
June 1 deadline that I am probably to run a bit over. I am
expecting work that isn't here yet. So.

Just not so easy to pick this up and go forward. Diary
tonight. Slowly beginning to feel Quincy again. Many old
friends in town. Surprising at first to hear they are finally
here, the not actually wanting to see some. Just so much

distance anymore. Hope to get close to Dan again.

5-30-72

Talked to Gerald tonight. Now, I'm watching dinosaurs hatch from eggs on the television. Hmm. And. A decision. A new piece. The name is to be *House*. There may be two additions, that is poems written after today that are included. Now, beginning with the work in this book, but not being able to use all of the things here. So far:

> Those Favorite
> The Magician's Apprentice
> The Chance
> Barbara
> The Bomber
> Journey
> Reference
> Home
> Ginger
> Revival
> Vita
> Baltimore

Still so new that it's soft. Not so sure of the edges. And a few of the poems above need some attention. So that they won't afterward. Just the need to draw so much in my life to an end. So as to start for the new. This decision in my verse is in keeping with my moving, my words with my body, Barbara, all. But this isn't distracting from the idea of piece event that I've talked of before. These poems sharing their character between themselves. And with a few things in *Circle* just as probably the next things. Too soon to talk about how these look next to any of *Lee*. Don't know how important that is anyway. I've felt these as more transitional since the beginning. Strength, always a question isn't it.

So, so. Talking tomorrow to the doctor who should set some limits as to what there is to be done. Hopefully, then I can begin settling. Last few days anxious. Of course. Getting on with these things.

6-8-72

Looks like my first entry in the study. Here upstairs. Busy times. Learning how to spend the day and not liking it, but necessary. ⅗s moved in this study, but not enough to make it comfortable. Enough to do letters and wade through this *december* thing. Lots of subscriptions coming in. Warm. I just seem to be getting through the days, weeks. Going fast. Barbara here in a week. Missing her badly.

6-19-72

Barbara gone yesterday after getting in very late Wednesday. Very hard visit on us. We wanted to see each other so much, it didn't click. Learned much. We're both pretty scared because we are both in love. I believe she is in love. So we parted with no plans, leaving it open. I have been feeling it pretty hard. I hope I can make the changes I need. Not exactly doing something new, but simply relaxing some things that in the course of weeks tightened. I have hopes. I've never given this much. It's more about me learning to let myself be loved.

So—with all this with Barbara comes the letter. From Stafford to Burns to me. Happy when it came, but I quickly forgot because of the situation. Now, looking at it, well, I am honored. He is certainly very kind. But when it comes to it, I wonder if the letter will have any relation to *Lee.*

6-20-72

Have decided today that I must get a place of my own. Everything suddenly pointed at the problem this has caused;

feel better already for having taken a step. Called Barbara, a bit under w/ sore throat. Not much to say, and I suppose shouldn't have expected. It's just that I had good news, and it was worth sharing. My not having my own place made *me* feel like a visitor. I'll be able to work, rest, and generally live better when I get this place. Not that it solves all, but a step. No, Barb will stay away from me for a time if not forever. She just won't get close; no way to change that either. I've just got to settle before anyone will get close, Barb or anyone.

Tried to land a nice store today with an upstairs apt. etc. But the men who owned it had already started remodeling. So, tomorrow I look again. Maybe a nice small house. Chris understands. Ridge knew it was coming. Guess I've spent enough time living on my own to want it that way again. Also a new poem:

For Robert E. Lee

I worry
that the
cats in
the afternoon
heat crawl up
in the engines
to the shade

all we try
as arts just
finding one
spot

6-19-72

Vita

since it all
happened once
at once

everything
since then our

own part
knowing this

Consciousness being God . . . the total sum of this planet knowledge. Music tree animal smell word touch earth making for the only pure music. This making self-knowledge the religion, most important form. Thus I suppose exposing me when I say science being of value, or deserving. But this kind of competition being equally as unfair here as in any other instance.

THIS: awareness in all its forms (way) is being that which is our most God-like characteristic. Thus all spiritual: plant, mineral, all living creatures. Have I covered it? All.

For me here specifically, poetry as consciousness. Plenty of room. *Robert E. Lee* my first book, first attempt to emulate consciousness via language. Earlier with hand, mouth, walk. Now word. All that I leave out here social convention.

Sounds like too much bullshit. Spiritual. Well.

6-23-72

Love Song

the accident
with the machine
or road

something set
anyday

*

I would cut
my hand
off it then
free   make
a hole in
my neck to breathe

but then to
be found there
or short of the
house by the
buildings

Should have word on getting the house by Monday.
Also looking into the possibility of a one-shot grant from an
individual here for funding enough to run me & *Salt Lick* for
a year. That would open up new possibilities for sure. Also
take some pressure off me. No word from Barbara.

6-28-72

Waiting Word From Barbara

the truth
either way
we will know
now

he said we
would all be
burned we had
to leave our house

this all in the
kitchen with black jesus
christ at the table

6-29-72

Precision

each door   all
windows
to see the falling
glass

7-3-72

Have had a great time these last few days. Large crowd here and lots of strangers. Sat. was a great find of a swimming place. Finally. I've been looking for four years. This one some mile/half on North Bottom Road past the fork— then left on the first well-traveled road going over the levee. Got a bridge to jump over. Ten a jam yesterday with folks numbering about forty. Some people from Chicago, and Dick getting in late last night. Again today at Doc's about 4:00. Me, unattached except to the group. Barbara not interested in seeing me any longer. Fact. Getting way behind in work. Letters getting pretty thick around the desk. It's ok.

7-9-72
Kathy-Zip-Burke-John
& Browner

Still going in the same spirit as above with the day going by *very* fast. Spent yesterday covering about ⅓ the county looking for buildings or houses that I might be able to rent. Covered Liberty, Payson, Plainville, Kingston, and everything between! Sat out at Doc's eating strawberries and drinking milk. Good times. Also found out I need only ten quarter hours to finish at Antioch. More mail. Just seems that this all takes me away from those things pressing me the most. And getting a little closer to people again. And happy with a few of these last poems. I continue to admire "For Robert E. Lee" which is probably one of the best poems I've written in a long time. As it came quick. Sitting with Barbara on the bed. She didn't like it. No revision. Came like "Message To The Chief" as a unit, not wanting revision. Saw it well enough that first time. In "Precision" also feeling good to me. Have to give Bruce copies in this next letter. No word from Gerald lately. May call today.

RING. Telephone. Browner. He has food. Says it's left over after his mother had the Quincy Cubs over. Hmmm.

8-8-72

So much between this last entry and now. Mostly the days getting by themselves. Have found a place and worked these past few days and today fixing an office. Auction last night. A visit from Barbara which went well. Still seeing Kathy. Much happened. Refusing pressure of most all types which has led to my not seeing much of the 5th Street crowd lately. Those people drifting now, and I doubt if the apts. will even be in use past this summer. I had the feeling that they were leaning on me for things to do. So, things pass. Rascal to live upstairs in the new place: 629 North 13th.

8-9-72

Still very busy with the new place. Office ready for transfer of my study from Chris's. It seems to be moving steadily. Getting up early for a big yard sale in Mendon tomorrow. Working longer each day and feeling good because of it. Have been thinking lately that as soon as I can sit down and finish *House*, I will send it to Godine. Also like to get a copy of *Lee* to him too. He seems pretty receptive to things in general; a kind note in response to my first letter. And Burns offering to send a letter in my behalf. Wish I could get Godine and Gerald together. No word from Gerald lately except a small card saying he liked the idea of *House* and really liked "For Robert E. Lee" and parts of the others from a long letter I sent last month late. And one night, I called. Silly on the phone as usual. I wonder that he even has one since everytime I call, he falls to pieces on the phone.

Saw a fine concert the other night in Iowa: Muddy Waters, Freddy King, and Z. Z. Top. Great.

8-22-72

First entry in a bit I see. Just busy with trying to make the house liveable. Pretty much have it in order. Still sewing carpet samples together. May paint the kitchen yet. And finally able to sit down with my journal and put *House* together. As it stands, the order:

> Those Favorite
> The Magician's Apprentice
> The Bomber
> Journey
> Reference
> Toll   —broke the one poem into
> Home   two.
> Revival
> The Chance
> Calico For Gladine
> Ginger
> Love Song
> For Robert E. Lee

It's good. Will get a copy off to Gerald and Godine w/ letters today. I think that compared to the other cycles, it is still very much the same but with a new door as well. Very pleased with the three in a row of *Home-Revival-The Chance* because of where it's sitting. Everything around the words making the poem as much as anything. —This cycle as the others written before I actually saw it in the poems— also most of the poems in the order of their appearance. Ending with the poem for Lee might be seen as a very contrived act, but the facts are that it was one of the last poems written; it does what "The Circle" did for *Circle,* and what more appropriate than a look at most all I've done to the time. Levels to work on for sure, but still placing most importance on the literal. And *Lee* my favorite poem of late. Came in a sitting over at Chris's one night. Maybe I'll send a copy to Stafford.

8-30-72/12:30 AM

Really tired from a long day w/ Castelaz who is fighting to get off campus and into QC. Very draining. Now Steve and Peggy here w/ Dan Luecking and a cousin, Paul. Too many some days. I guess this kegger coming up worries me too. Kegger-Jam. Everything happening so fast.

Work to begin in earnest on the next *Salt Lick* as soon as I get back from Texas. Want to leave on or by Sept. 10th and be back in six days.

Card from Gerald says he thinks *House* is the best I've done. Good though, I still have doubts about inclusion of "Ginger." He received a copy without it and liked it that way. Didn't say whether he would write Godine or not. I'm having trouble thinking much about this because of the situation here.

9-2-72

Rain. 59 degrees. Wind. Looks like we call the jam off. Which in some ways takes a load off. Have to try to do it next weekend. Cold, miserable day. Have to spend it inside somewhere. Monroe in town for it and won't make it next week. The gypsy was right.

9-5-72

Sent a copy of *House* to Stafford today. Also one to Joe Ribar at Figtree Press to see if he is interested in putting it out. And a few poems taken by *The Expatriate Review:* "Barbara" and "Near Liberty, Illinois." —Getting things in order before my trip to Texas this Sunday. Much to do here in the office including the proposal for renewal of the federal grant. It won't be considered until after the new year, unless it is in very soon. Need money for the next issue. Well, working on it. Believe I will ask for a flat $2000 this time. Don't see where I can go wrong. Will include copies of reviews of this last issue which may wield some weight. Long day.

9-11-72
Whitney, Texas

Got in last night about 11:30. Long drive for sure. Dropped Kathy off in St. Louis. Good to see the family again; and amazed at all they have done here. House more or less done with bits left to finish.

New Home

in Whitney, Texas
no grass but sand
and rock front
yard

looking for the
sissors one drawer
second drawer I
run across the
bottom half of an
egg carton my
mothers taken for
a jewlery case

9-16-72
Whitney, Texas

Have been enjoying this visit home more than any for so long, partly due to my family being more content with themselves and their surroundings than ever before. Spent some time visiting David Searcy in Dallas, two evenings. First evening had a fine time. Met one of Burns's old students who is from Holland: Willem. Also saw Chaplin's *The Great Dictator.* Fantastic film. Just amazing. Sort of made David nervous, I think, because of being in the role of host, at least host to me. So, instead of spending the night I drove on home. Yesterday afternoon I saw him again briefly. He read *House* with interest. Things he said over the visit that stick in my mind would be "I've never wanted to rewrite anyone's work more than yours," and ". . . you have a sort of waxy invulnerability." Ha. I must say that his enthusiasm over *House* was heartening since he hit specifically many particulars I had in mind while doing the poems. He also noted the problem with the second stanza of "Toll" which I have been thinking of changing for a while. Ed Zahniser also mentioned it in a note. Will change it to read as it did in the original:

> . . .by the time the
> stories had been through
> the bars they had
> asked for more money
> and they got it

Reads better. Don't know why I made the entry in the final typeup as I did. Well. Better. David also seeing an interesting similarity between the word/weight/cadence of "Calico" and WCW's poem "Fine Work with Pitch and Copper."

9-24-72

Home for almost a week. Most of the time spent trying to get over the drain of travel. If I had rested the day after the return all would have gone well. As it was, I didn't and have been dragging for the last three days. Letter and tape from Burns. Excellent tape aside from his nervous apologies. Says "I'll only do a half hour" and does both sides of the cassette full. Burns. One thing did strike me in particular though: he said I worry about my reputation. I suppose it is true enough, though I am not unconscious of the fact which is why it shows in letters and tapes. The rejection by Godine and no word from H&R have brought this to the surface. Also the position I find myself in of not going to one sort of school or another in the fall for the first time I can recall. Being at loose ends with my time and with those around me. Having little patience w/ Kathy. Seems the best course for me to pursue is not sending out any ms. once those out return. Then turn my attentions to the office and magazine. Much to do as the time of the new issue rolls in. Must turn my energies back in on myself for strength. Seems that that which I have been casting returns with less than it went. Not an excuse, but fact.

9-28-72

Cold in my office. This winter may be to do as Gerald suggests and write with mittens on . . . returned *Letters* to him today at his request which I do/don't understand. In some ways, feel that this is tied in to the reputation business which I regret since in the end, I feel as I've been weak. Disappointed others. As a result, not sending ms. back out. Should let that sort of thing rest at least until this next issue of *Salt Lick* out. Just more or less started figuring pages today. Suppose I should have done it before now, but to be honest, didn't trust anyone with it. Ridge going to do some of it, and Schweda mentioned a woman here who is doing his dissertation. Well. Get her to do some of it.

Going through a long piece by Bruce Andrews for this issue which has some nice passages, though suggest revision. Seems that the work he and Ron Silliman and Coolidge to a lesser extent is more of a technical innovation meant for the reader in general rather than particular; simply pointing back to word weight. Good enough I suppose as a means, but I will be disappointed if it goes no further. See this as directly related to the minimal concept but no more important than that. Liberating for a change, but for me simply making the stakes for a traditionalist verse higher; for linear lines to overcome the temptation of this word/object verse, there must be an honesty that has been there all along and only lately obscured by the flood of second-rate work. Of course it is tempting, because it looks so easy, but there will only be a few masters. Just as Creeley with his verse: the model for the last ten years of look-alike. Hell, look at mine. I worried and rightfully so. Get the feeling that this is of even less value. Better working in the yard.

10-6-72
1 AM

Working more lately the envelopes and new *Salt Lick*. New new. After one long night with Dan. Covers front and back. The questions are between creating a front of new symbols, thin in two rows, Dan w/ that one.  Hard to get serious enough w/ the symbols we have come up with so far. Still kicking a colored sticker or decal around; bowl of fruit. Have to check the price of that one, but more or less committed to the idea of going on with this issue as 1&2, Volume 2. Seeing a new turn because of most all factors. First ten numbers completed; back in Quincy again; new stance on larger bodied work; Dan back and active again; feelings of newness which isn't far from what every issue felt. Just more this time. Even more of a break after the last issue; it making big steps away, but this one just that much further down the way of travel. *Because of the last one,* this issue with a new source to begin, and so on. Remaining open to the new place only seen upon entering. A way.

way of seeing   new place
every situation

Olson's "Field of Force" at work. Reading *Letters For Origin 1950–1956* and am surprised at the Olson, in *Salt Lick* via Gerald. He's been after me to read this for some while but only now at it. Some of it bitchy, but much glorified common sense. On the page. Great Olson. Would have been interesting to have seen some of Corman's letters.

10-13-72

To leave in a few hours for KC to visit with Slater. Randy going also; be glad to see Robert since it's been some while, but glad to get back to Quincy. Quick trip earlier this week to Champaign to see Larry Coryell & Four Play. Great just great. Steve Marcus, Marvin Bronson, Mike Mandell, Harry Wilkenson. Only $1. Went with Bill Browner. Amazing how artists of such caliber almost starve for lack of work outside NYC.

Making more definite decisions on this new *Salt Lick.* Have decided to put *House* in this one as a result of long letter exchange with GB. After moving some distance from the original motives and ideas of the magazine, I then consciously considered my work only if there was little time and space to fill. Not wanting to subject myself to the same sort of contempt that I feel for so many editors who put their work alongside the wonderful simply because of their position. But putting my work in this issue is the result of a rather ruthless logic that holds only truth as sacred. I know now that I have been working on a double-standard with my work on one side with the magazine on the other. The now obvious shortcomings of this system have no doubt been the cause of much of the personal difficulties the past year. Honesty would have my relation to my verse *and* my magazine as the same. And it shall be. Thus the inclusion of *House* in the new issue because it is as strong if not stronger than the company it keeps. I believe this. It is to leave the judgment of the work by an editor who includes his among those he publishes to the only truth: the work. All the others, reasons in circumstances, circumstances for criticism; where it, is when. These less than the work. Of course in cases, these circumstances lend much to the making of the work. But I can't get past the ultimate of work as conceived. Under this all else.

10-13-72
Restaurant in Missouri

After Leaving The House

I turn in the
drive that
leads further
back
    knowing
the time where
I am living
will change

just as the
road pea gravel
shoulders on
either side

*

from all the
leaving and back
again

it is finally
to know one road

10-17-72

Finished the preceding poem begun in a cafe in Missouri with Randy. Fine visit with Slater in KC. Narrow es-
ᵣ ᵣ ᵣ ᵣ bust just as leaving with smoke. —Letter from GB
work by Trammell. Long poem series, thus 8 to 9
uld be good.
ᵢ paper today for the new issue . . . moving to a
finish for cover; 60lb offset inside; bond 20lb linen
Gerald's *Minuet,* and 9lb blue manifold for divid-
ᵧ/book insert. Also finished a second draft revision
ᵤce. Issue getting more visible every day. Going to lay
ᵢ*M* tomorrow morning. Maybe start shooting Friday.
ᵤld writing much lately and Dan in conversation both
ᵣelping as I've been going rough with examination of self
and magazine last week. Seeing them as eventually the same
concern or relevant to the same concerns. Dealing as well as
I can with everything I have done to this point, curious to be
so unconcerned with parts as I want to be. Trying to look
once at it all. This leading me to reading or rereading again.
Actually, probably little rereadings as I'm not reading much
for passing time. Just those few questions.

10-27-72

Feeling pretty numb, sore throat, etc., taking over my
body and thoughts. Such wet weather here of late forcing
me in for the day tomorrow and maybe the night. Also have
to lay off this smoke.
Get a chance to do a letter for Gerald. Hopefully pull a

Ezra Pound dies at 87, hailed as literary giant

VENICE, Italy (UPI) — Poet Ezra Pound is dead at 87, the last and possibly greatest giant of a fabulous literary era which embraced such friends and disciples as Ernest Hemingway, T. S. Eliot, James Joyce, William Butler Yeats, Robert Frost and D. H. Lawrence.

Critics and writers hailed him as a pioneer in reshaping the language of the 20th century English even as they deplored or assailed his political beliefs, a muddled mixture of anti-Semiticism, fascism and fundamentalist economics that caused him to be indicted for treason in World War II, confined to a mental hospital for 13 years and then self-exiled to his beloved Italy.

"He outlived them all, all of them," said novelist James Dickey. "With his death an era comes full circle."

Pound died Wednesday night in a Venice hospital, two days after his 87th birthday and 24 hours after doctors admitted him for treatment for an intestinal blockage. His long-time companion, Mrs. Olga Rudge, was at his side.

Pound was the only American poet included in the recently published New Oxford Book of English Verse.

He shaped the poem which later became Eliot's masterpiece, "The Wasteland," persuaded a publisher to take a chance on a Joyce novel entitled "Ulysses." He discovered Frost, influenced Yeats—Pound was his secretary—and helped gain an audience for

EZRA POUND

poet Ford Madox Ford.

But at his death, Pound was a man without a country, an enigmatic exile forever fixed in the American mind as a disloyal madman who broadcast propaganda for Fascist dictator Benito Mussolini and spewed messages of hate to Jews.

They were activities which brought him indictment, but never a formal charge, of treason by a U.S. grand jury.

He never recanted the political beliefs which sent him to jail and an insane asylum—St. Elizabeth's Hospital in Washington, D.C.—for 13 years, until Frost, Hemingway, Eliot and poet Archibald MacLeish convinced Washington to free him to return to Europe.

He returned unrepentant to Italy in 1958, where he greeted newsmen with a stiff-armed

Fascist salute and proclaimed: "All America is an insane asylum."

Pound spent the rest of his life in the German-speaking Alpine town of Merano, the home of his daughter, Mary, or in Venice, with occasional trips to Spoleto and the Italian Riviera.

He rarely spoke to outsiders and after suffering a heart attack in 1962, he worked only fitfully on what some critics consider his most ambitious project—"The Cantos," 120 of them, modeled on Dante's "Divine Comedy."

In his most productive years, Pound wrote some of the most inventive poetry of this century and edited the writings of other poets, sharpening them into what critics called masterpieces by proxy.

Pound won dozens of honors, one of them the prestigious Bollingen Prize awarded in 1949 by the U.S. Library of Congress. Ironically, he won it while confined in the Washington asylum.

Only this year a panel of writers nominated him for the annual Emerson-Thoreau Medal awarded by the American Academy of Arts and Sciences. The academy voted against giving him the award, chiefly because of his political beliefs.

Pound was born Oct. 30, 1885, in Hailey, Idaho, the only child of a civil servant who later rose to assistant assayer in the U.S. Mint. His father also minted his own money briefly until ordered to stop.

few of these feelings about Olson together essentially though *Letters For Origin* this time. Beautiful the way he comes out of the fuzz to the clear, *CLEAR;* sunburst. Never outshines, or tries, but reflect that he's seen, his genius. An ability to see such great systems even in action (update). Feel like a little anthro. reading just to stand a little closer. Yet, without any rereading of Olson verse, still feeling that sense of failure of his verse. His problem of standing on his verse and ethic (poetic) without falling off. Inconsistent inside; but have the urge to stop this line of thought until through *Human Universe* collection of essays completely. Also *Mayan Letters.*

Rough-out on the magazine to be done this weekend. Not certain of the size as yet, but including *House* for certain. Firm on that. Dan thinks it a mistake, or he can't imagine himself doing such which presents the flaw in that line of thinking: trading places, etc. or final fact of the impossible jump! Individual with event. Each breathing and cold as it will be finally above us.

11-2-72

Happened while Dan and I were in St. Louis—funny that the day after (today) I received Gerald's copy of *Cantos*—also collected earlier WCW and Zukofsky *All.*

The days full and going surprisingly fast. A day drive to St. Louis in the rain. Dan bringing up an interesting point of the cyclical form the Chinese see time in. Moving out of a non-linear stance. I have not heard of this; wonder at it, but the point in my seeing my work in their cyclical sense that afternoon. Each being a record of a distance or duration with a particular character (to the work) being the calling card. This event being legislated by that which exists independently of me, my working toward. The ENERGY. Facing it through only realizing it as an end to the cycle, but working with a most general awareness of the fact. *Circle* as example of sounded work, levels within, the final poem being my source of final knowing, its identity. Having just done the thing and then the record. Each cycle being to itself essentially with all "informing (GB)" each other but standing where they will be. Where each will.

Splitting hairs on a point would have *The Circle* as the first poem of that next cycle or possibly an independent. Just the feeling that there is an artificiality at just times where it being after the fact of the cycle. As postscript, but in that poem I was realizing during it, the poem as act of recognition as well as marking time.

Pick up *House.* Different ordering with the poems out of chronological sequence. Mostly as I did less in the way of false starts, ending with *For Robert E. Lee.* Exactly where I was: looking again at all I have and placing it up again as faith. Always the possibility of setting it down. That. Can't see past it now. Tireless honesty, the truth with the only faith that it will be. There are no mistakes. There is a fact and then those around it. —The same place on the new issue only with some typing done. Give more to Ridge tomorrow.

11-9-72

Rain to sleet outdoors.

Figured the covers last night with Dan. To be speckled silver, as well, for which I built a screen today—screen wire. Now to find a silver silkscreen ink as the aluminum paint I experimented with today being of an oil base made stains on the back of the test covers. —Half of the paper for *BM* missing from an order mixup. Expected tomorrow. Spent five hours stripping negatives for the book. Looks good. Good.

Because at given instances, I know that and where I am. For these even brief flashes, knowing at that stop time and this event from which direction work. "Home," "The Circle," "Lee," "Message To The Chief." Some of the more directional of the poems and their current. At times speaking in definition. See Gerald's work as very self-definitive. Telling not only what it is, but what it isn't; how to read it, and whether he thinks in terms of audience. *Boccherini's Minuet* drier than *Letters* and I'm not talking simply out of the larger choice in *LTOM. BM* serving as document to the event that *Letters* is. History for his systems.

11-12-72

Have scratched the individual speckling of covers because of a lack of a silver substance with a nonoil base; stains through the covers this way. Will run a silver plate with two others: one for the cover lettering and one for the logo and lines on the back. Will fold *BM* tomorrow looks like. Hope to finish with it this week if possible with some layout in the magazine. Waiting on new fiction from David who also did an appreciation for Gerald: Gerald Burns's Nouns. Will hold that for the next issue along with *Peter Rabbit's Trick.*

Sound as seeing on the page

Seems in arrival in conversation that I may get just that much closer to the poem which is as real in its use of words, that the words are what they are: self-definition. Again the poem which is itself, relation to poet as seen *separate.* Sound was the means by which I made this move. The tool for the door. Poem constructs or what we can pull from the air, our language, diet, and other systems of things.—may be doing a small thing about Michael's work for this one as I don't particularly like the one Drake did for me.

11-15-72

Not as down today because of the setbacks on *BM.* Not only does the cover (first sheet) have to be rerun (my choice/half my fault) but two other sheets as well. The "s" on the end of the word Illinois runs over the fold into the front of the cover. No choice in the matter finally; could not pull it out. And now in collating I find that there is offset that ruined two other sheets. Told Bert that I could not put that out either, to which he agreed (Gus's fault). Slater, Ann Darr, Bruce Andrews, Ron Silliman, drawing/poem/pages by Lee DeJasu, Stephen Leggett, a few others and *House* in the magazine.

11-19-72

Eleven pages of the magazine laid out. Pick up more copy tomorrow which leaves me two days before leaving with Dan for Chicago. All pages in the "Essays/Notes" section. Happy that that section is breathing again. This issue gives me faith to believe that it is the thing you can do (allow for) that occurs almost more naturally than mere correspondence. The mix. Letters there when they *arrived* there. At least it gets away from the joke, insult, crack column that most I've seen fall to, especially *Kayak.* Even *Seventies,* though seeing itself as *the more serious.*

Have finished three mystery box drawings which I'm very happy with. Some question on this third one, but still hope to do more with these after the issue.

Confronting more format changes as we see them. Evolving constantly as whole. Press-on-letters for the names and headings as they are much cheaper than set letters. Going to rearrange the contents page. Handle page numbers differently. This new one to be the new home base as format. Can see possibly fewer changes in the whole for the next one. Fitting aimed at being the form which imposes less on its contents while still existing as FORM. Whole, as single.

11-28-72

Just about ¾s of the magazine layed up now. Some needing only page numbers to be completed, camera-ready. Dan and I still to do this thing for Michael. Both of us to fill a single page. Short on space and the nature of what I want to do is in itself the short space. To use the base of the "Intro For Michael" I did for the reading we did in West Virginia.

David Armstrong to come down this weekend to do a silkscreen for the issue. He has done some fine constructions that I had a chance to see on the visit to Chicago; Dan's for Thanksgiving.

Playing much. Percussion, drums when I get down to 5th St. Made some tapes at Jerry Dean's with John and Dicky. Surprisingly good.

12-2-72

Very late and exhausted after such a long day. Got started on the folio for this issue; Steve Armstrong and Sonny got in late the night before. —We switched from the idea of doing two silkscreens to something much larger in scope. We are doing a painting which is roughly 19′ × 19′ composed of 7″ × 7″ pieces of paper (28lb ledger stock—white). Spray paint. Each square is being numbered, one to go with each *Salt Lick*. Also have to document the facts that go with this event; a page to go w/ it. Wondering about the possibility of getting a photo of the completed piece (composite). First three panels done, top to bottom. Hope for an early start tomorrow to get as much done as possible, since Steve will be gone by early evening. —Feeling to be working

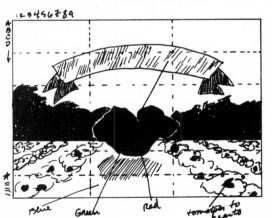

on such a scale and yet taking care with each individual square. —Space and interest from George Irwin.

12-3-72

Again late, but six panels completed today. Dan and I did two after that. Really taking shape, but the hardest part just ahead. Problem of cost of spray paint to be solved also. Will try to get three more done in the week and finish next weekend. All this while still the last pages to type and lay up, finish Gerald's book, and begin stripping the negatives for the magazine. Trying to get in full days. Eat and rest well. Best I can. Will get a copy of Gerald's book to him in the mail tomorrow—just to let him know it exists. I mean running late, and he has waited; get at least a copy together for him.

12-11-72

Twelve of the panels for the painting done now, which amazes. Last three this week. Dan seems to think well on his feet, and knows it. Should with this piece open to a new area. Strikes me as original; the breadth of the event with well defined sense of documentation and participation. I imagine the piece he writes for it to be good also.

Gerald, happy with the book, called to talk the other night. The hard part of promotion over now as I got copies to *Books In Print,* etc. Running short of extra copies because the printer's helper keeps making errors. Sent Gerald 20. Issue looking like after Christmas now. Contributing factor being bulk mailing permit for '73. And again care instead of hurrying the final details for no just reason. Start printing the magazine in the morning. Still some copy to do. Also Antioch credit deadline beginning to be a headache. Deadline today I found out in a flyer I received today. Hello.

12-22-72
Whitney, Texas

Much of the final copy work done for the issue before leaving Thursday, shortly before noon. 14½ hour drive. The painting finished, FIRST POSITION OF THE HEART (Dan's), and photographed before leaving which is a big load over, too. Turned out really well, though the missed registration between panels, which was clear as of seeing the piece whole for the first time, bothersome. Very impressive though. Hope the photos turn out well.

Seems that this time home here, Texas, I am more aware of the beauty of how people, we, place ourselves toward our living. Strikes me that this is where much of my verse originates, only as isolated events. Some leading to the wider sight. "Those Favorite" more direct than a "Conversation" still some persist in calling it "the human condition" for lack of freedom. Imagination, but the beauty there in the facts.

> *Heart*
>
> it is the first
> time to know
> that it is
> living here in
> these houses
> things weve made
> with us   taking
> what we know
> first our eating
> and love at least
> as seriously as
> the rest
>   finally
> lying down to
> know from this

                   place there are
                   no mistakes the
                   time some would say

                                                    for Dan
         Just trying to see it pure, a way he would.

Christmas Day

"I'm the one that do the hitting," mother said after the small scuffle brought her in to ride the two boys. To preserve something. The younger of the two who had earlier, before leaving the room, turned the set on, came back. The station different and he didn't like it. Turned it. The older, a year, slapped him but only after he threatened. He must have known the situation wouldn't change: the station would not be put back.

But his anticipation to the event. His appetite, not hunger, but his following in his part of the history. How much learned? And the younger's crying or protests meant more for those outside the room than his brother, the situation, his own part.

The mother knowing this, or if not all, enough. Entering the room, but not; standing in the door. Then sitting by neither of the boys, being there to herself.——

Actually, the above just some side effect after reading most of the pieces in Creeley's *Gold Diggers* here on the visit. Call from David Searcy breaking the piece. A stopping place at any rate. The reading making fiction particularly attractive, though not the usual looking easy . . . such subtle formalism though, barely visible out from under the cautiousness. His correctness. There is here a great introduction to his verse; up to *Pieces.* I don't feel there is any real fiction I could do now; seems it would be watered down verse w/ instructions and including half of what I think en route to the poem that strikes me as interesting, but finally not important (or those connections that as important to me, useless on the page). Just not seeing the fiction in my living now, may never. Not to be regretted; simply hasn't happened. Strikes me curious that I still would return to the moral in an entry in this journal. Recently reread first pages of same again and *almost* embarrassed. A year of movement. To see David Wednesday afternoon before leaving.

12-27-72

Nice short visit with David today. More or less set to do his book for the next in the series, *Peter Rabbit's Trick.*

Also spent some time with Nanny and Grandaddy before leaving. They keep on. Got some of the family photos from them. Hope someone gets the rest of them put in a book since they keep them in a sack.

Ticket

> each of the different
> houses where Johndaddy moved
> the family would soon
> take the same
> features   morning glories to
> front porch razor strap
> over the front door
> radio Bible the car
> white clapboard green
> trim more of tan than
> not   children leaving
> in order   Gladine packing
> tomatoes just after
> high school to see
> Ft. Worth

1-5-73

First entry after the trip home. New year. Moving pretty fast since then and only getting slowed down a bit now. The magazine half folded and the rest soon. Finally to finish copy this weekend. More trouble with paper shortage, re-order. Gus ruined another half-run on a page. Don't know how long he is going to remain. Want this issue to pull itself together since getting little ease. The wait. More letters, ". . . when?" Dan having some trouble getting going. Didn't get illustrations in Chicago, did none. Resists having to work at this rate/pressure. Myself as well. So close. "Heart" title for poem.

1-16-73

All the magazine in print. As of yesterday. Still the portfolio and subscription things to do, but the magazine *in print.* Hand coloring taking up the time and energy now. Logo on 2nd page and boy on contributors' page getting colored; one page with just fruit which is Dan's. I think we may do that one with watercolor depending on how it affects the paper. Also the glue in (tipped in illustrated panel of shells). Cover came out really well with some last minute attention; addition of more black and a frame. Otherwise, graphically a very loose issue. We would have eliminated the silver outside the frame if we had seen it beforehand, but must realize that an issue will be as free as its cutoff point. The reason this one so hard longer is that we left the end point floating, to be set during the processes; part finished, part not. Worked well enough this time.

Again find myself in a position toward the issue of not knowing how it will be received because of my closeness, which I neither think good or bad as it's simply a fact. Points could be made with either coloring. I am almost certain that the issue would have been impossible if I had been living elsewhere, or had held myself to the issue in any less of a discipline.

Barbara here in a surprise visit this weekend. Good. Easy. Put things away for a few days; good since I was pretty low about finances. Just got the official papers for the new federal grant. This time $1,000 only on a matching basis. No help from Geo. Irwin. Ridge back yesterday and help from Chris, brighter looking today.

Little time for letters or verse or anything but the magazine, but soon through. Letter from Gerald who says he has enjoyed himself with pre-pub *BM*. Got copies to Zukofsky and Dahlberg. Miss the work with Gerald. Happy for him. David and Lally only replies to *BM* yet. David of course loved it. Michael attracted, but to sit with it for a bit. The best way to take Gerald's work, strikes me, picking it up, setting it down. Living with it for a time. Otherwise the strength missed.

1-23-73

At a breathing spell. 250 magazines stapled without book, trim to go. The rest still in the works. Have been keeping at it pretty solid. Getting several hours a day in—also coloring taking the most time now. Also have a bit more time with it as my course doesn't start till Feb. 22. Portfolio the thing left to take the work now. In spite of the cost, we will have to print a slide of the painting (color) in order to complete the presentation. Without it the idea would be taken less seriously than it would otherwise, still less than deserved. Looks like it will mean another $100. Resolution of the portfolio and envelopes still to be done. Envelopes to be speckled and sprayed. To be done with speckly screen I built earlier and stencils. Red and deep blue. Silver speckles after the cover.

So, by the weekend, 250 started will be complete. Work on up to say 500 for an initial mailout. Must say I am proud of this one.

Here doing laundry. A very beautiful nurse is drying her clothes and is pleasant to watch. White uniforms. Direct movement toward her work. Folding the clothes. Some hung, from the way of it, she will leave soon.

2-5-73

Birthday. Just back from overnight in Peoria with Dick Vonachen & family. Nice party, surprise, from Dan. 23.

The issue begins to be over; I can begin to see past it. Good. Few things begin to fall to their space. Should hear about the slides for the portfolio this week. 200 more copies of the magazine ready to staple.

Lifetime

for the one
of me which believes
all others   closer
to than not

it is a day

2-7-73

Snow today. Three inches. And some disappointment with getting funds for the magazine. Trying not to sound despondent; the facts of financing have always been this way. Looks like I will have to scrape to simply get the $1,000 matching.

Waiting still for the print for the portfolio. Still think we can be in the mail by the end of the month.

New McLaughlin album just beautiful. Especially "Sanctuary" which is of such classical proportions that I am amazed at each hearing.

Sanctuary

all the travel from
and to it   now known
now there   these
gifts as better the
things we need

I believe the time in
each as the sun
new sun   star is
is here

Just as talking with Randy. The piece as the first realization that there is no sanctuary (safety) as that, but knowing this becomes the sanctuary. Living with, rather than the regardless. But to this first knowing, again the myth of safety as we are taught. It is saddening. Momentarily a place, where some turn ahead, and some no more. Gerald who says "What doesn't add subtracts" is true enough to this point. After this, all adds. The point of no mistakes. Guilt falling from us.

2-13-73
2:30 AM

Long interview with a reporter for the paper here in Quincy who is doing a feature on the press. Would hope this to bring a few more people to my class. Slow pre-enrollment. Of course, almost expect to get burned.

Things sorting slowly. Should get to some of the envelopes for this week. No word on the slides. Caught up on letters these few days for the first time in a stretch.

Two Days

now of drizzle
light fog on

the town

to this all
until this
evening

and then a spoon
from the soup
for the cat

2-15-73

Very cold and snow. This winter so active compared to most; flu all around. Letter from Gerald w/ 133–136 *Letters* very fine. 133–134 both seeming to be the first letters to approach sex (regard) sensually. Beautiful and am glad to see again what I had begun to see earlier: a warmer poem, a poet that would touch rather than poke or sweet. Not that the poems have changed to the page; just the particular words which at their point are humane. Brief review from *Chicago Review* of *SWR.* Summer, notes. "A standout is G.B.'s Boccherini's Minuet . . . almost musical poem." Of course Gerald liked that. About time.

2-25-73

Article appeared in HW here terrible. Beyond the expectable misquotes and "He is a poet . . ." they made no mention of Dan or Steve and Randy. After I made it quite explicit that it was not a one-man operation. Apologized to Dan, but what good after the fact. Wrote letters to both the reporter and the editor, the latter of them hopefully to be in the letter column. Make the corrections.

First class met at the school. Still need a few more paying students to make it go. Not a bad first one. Schweda being so much; his having done so much to make it go while I try to get out from under here at the house.

Bought a clock today for $4. It as part of my trying to pull some order into things. Not eating or sleeping well—of course it follows that I get less work done and what is done sometimes suffers. Not pleased with much of this recent verse, but believe moving some of the chores out and with spring coming, things will improve. Long winter. Days long time.

2-28-73

Consciousness as a matter of dimension. The young history man here at the college whose paper on the activists of the 60's found that these "individuals" felt that they were extending things done by their parents which should come as no surprise. Not that generation or any other has successfully or by natural act been able to actually stand aside from their history, the folks, the rest.

And yet in time, what has preceded and what we anticipate are but equal to each. To itself, all time. That plain. Where all is en route and yet there.

3-17-73

About to Chicago for a reading; Notre Dame High School, one day through McDonell, $100. Long drive and I'm not away.

Talking to Dan it has finally shown itself to me that the departure McLaughlin's music is making for its family, of music: that each piece exists seemingly apart from, of itself, situations that exist at the same time as others. But to different.

3-25-73

Brian Smelser buried yesterday. It was a great shock learning of his death as I just got in the door from Chicago. Trip leaving me very tired, just caught me flat. Only four days before he died I got a warm, happy letter from him.

Having died from an OD—heroin in Mexico, body held at the border, rumors, this all unsettling. But then the funeral. At the grave as the priest concluded his piece saying we have heard the last from Brian, there was a long, piercing highball call from a train some distance away—which was too long, very long until we knew it was him.

Now trying to pull some things to some sort of close. Getting up to clinch the issue. This, the journal being the only running thread throughout the work. Nothing as Burns's; I gather from "Homage" and tape that he in journal work polishes, sculpts, and skips rope. Classical approach even if we have to see him in history (classical being of a pure source some many times removed). Of course correct operating *his* history.

Journal

until an idea will
be known by   as people

which is to work
to say what is not
as stance or yourself
held toward all

the garden must wait
the ground wet and
would nothing but go
to clods if turned now
this spring

—3-14-73

Much too much rain.

4-1-73

Still catching my breath after the quick trip to Chicago. CCLM party at by the Playboy Towers was as it was. Saw Curt Johnson after a few years, talked to Anania a bit, met a few people. Not that we would have missed much besides free drinks if not there, but good for. Also good excuse to get up for more jazz. Saw a great set by Donald Byrd. Side men great as if not more impressive than Byrd: Billy Harper, Joe Chambers, Eric Barnes. Beautiful. (Didn't say, but last trip finally saw Tony Williams which was a long standing dream, his genius.)

Rain, rain, rain, rain. Flooded Mississippi and worse all the streams, tributaries which have risen from their banks and now many fields under. Water everywhere. First hot day everything will bloom.

Letter from Gerald about journal as form. Which, though I address myself to that stance now, I can not see much past. Journal as life work would tend to be the sum of all the areas one *would* work in, those failures fitting here, the poems happening just along the way, but I didn't say accident. Burns finding after a few misgivings the idea possible, though the thing WCW touches in *Imaginations.* Now, I can say that the poems and pieces of homework which might happen to precede or follow will make the book, this allowing editing of a sort. The question of *all* being for book I can't see well enough. Journal as stance *toward,* even the idea creeping into *Salt Lick,* or better there my just beginning to catch.

4-4-73

Calf Town

or the south side
more German   the
cars drive slower

living north you
would see fewer
taverns the less
kids not as many
blond families

my being back has
me here

a year may
yard work and printers
devil

4-5-73

Roadside Artists

there was money made
everytime the ground cracked
open all the pulloff stands or a
family in a car with honey
and carnival glass to the
highway shoulder

fourteen white tables
at the melon stand
cheniel bed spreads to a
line at the side   going
a little with the wind
we always ate at home

where there was more
since we fixed it for
ourself   never us the
people in the stand

Michael to come in, and we read Sunday at Quincy College. Maybe Anselm Hollo to come through also. —To St. Louis tomorrow to haul furniture for Chris. Should be a long day.

4-21-73

The poem finally of the life it would. The first never sitting as I knew it would. The tie with T. Williams work a true one. But knowing through all that that makes me unclear on myself, at times. It also serves to say a kind thing to Gerald; proves the man who believes in the pleasing quality of cleanly stacked dishes or folded linen in a closet has a place of the world.

Lifetime

for the one
of me which believes
all others   closer
to than not it
is a day it
is a day for
cleaning

would there
be another of the
one who invented
the stairs for himself
first but for the family

Rain and high wind for two days. If we get much more rain, the corn crop will probably take a beating. No corn in yet, few fields even broken. Obvious the effect of this on the town as well as the country, only natural though as we all depend on it for something. Possibly the mutual benefit of all. My garden late getting in to the rain, but suspect it affects only me. I am not a farmer, nor great contender. The garden is the thing left in the western man that carried over from the gatherers. Look at the plants in the cities, around the buildings.

4-23-73

Worst flood in our written history. Through the night and day, levees at La Grange, Canton, and West Quincy broken. Water to Taylor. 28.5 and climbing. Hannibal hit very hard with much of downtown in water to five feet. Bridges at Louisiana, Hannibal, Quincy, and Keokuk closed. When the levee on the Fabius River in West Quincy started to go, people on this side unable to help, stranded. Crowds in the parks watch, 300 in Riverview this afternoon. It's easy to forget that there is a river until it changes in such a large way, as to force us to alter to it.

4-26-73

Fresh asparagus, white potato, salad and it's supper tonight. Busy day at the shop, Bert waking me up this morning. Most of the people go back to work in spite of the flood though the many who worked in W. Quincy and in the factories along the river work around the house now, or hunt mushrooms. There is a river-made lake that's 13 miles long from just above LaGrange, Mo. to well south of Quincy and six miles wide to Taylor and that highway. Many buildings in the water crumbling. —Copy of *The Slate Notebook* from Gerald today. Looks very strong through the first few pages. *Salt Lick* out officially tomorrow. The portfolio getting done slowly, but that last bit. Actually done. Still the bulk of addressing & mailing to do but to be at that place with it after this long. Long enough to pick it up and run till wanting to rest, then on.

The show was very fine and I am glad to see Dan now

feeling a bit more easy with himself, feeling that he has done something, his own hardness with himself as it will be.

> The best bodyman in Dallas
> was the name he had
> for a while, but Jack Simon
> to his stationery, and the building.
> *Major* is what everybody
> knew though around the town
> he was born, or cut to *Maj*
> by Tom, his brother, my second
> father, my real father.

This part being that. Part to a long poem, not meaning to be simply autobiographical, but storytelling. What would be as immediate and personal for the telling as to those listening. I can see most of the work to now there, I can see all of the work there save those stepping out.

4-29-73

> *West Quincy Flood*
>
> spring flood time
> has rivermade a lake
> thirteen miles long through
> La Grange to well south
> of town and six miles
> across
>
> a time   town people
> on a bluff park
> over the waterland could
> see it crest
>
> the day the fence leans

away from the house
who built it

Not meaning to be light of the poor people of the flood. (Or the many who could have hauled out equipment, but did not.)

5-2-73

This spring continues to the assault. Tornado last night killed two in Kahokia, Mo., not far away, while an inch of rain and 40 mph winds had me running from door to window. Now yet another flood crest set for Friday, back up to 26 feet. Without this new rain and rain the disaster had already visited us. Illinois River getting out of its banks. Kampsville, Niota, Meradosia and town in Calhoun Co. all under different stages of flood water. The tributaries already swollen, the new rain has no place to go but into the fields. As much as half the corn crop may never get planted this year, while the late date for soy beans draws closer as well. To the south, cotton planters with the same problems.

Garden plot broken finally, but still needs tilling. $6 at a sale for spade, hoe, and dirt fork.

5-9-73
The Genius of the late
Lee Morgan.

This as piece for "Poem" and not stepping out to tell anyone the way Stafford in *Field* fell.

It was my intention to show what I meant with example, for the first poem. But not that, as much as a first poem. The idea was with Williams in mind, his only "Poem" as for the cat. Giving the example in a class at the Belvedere Hotel in Baltimore. A poem as true to the facts as the painting on cave wall. It came smoothly. Getting it down back at the apt. afterwards though Dan McD agreed that it was as close on the page as in that room, but it was something less than earlier. More than the invention (movement gone) since having a poem to paper also is an invention, though their own. It is the difference between the hunt, and the painting. The hunt, yes; who can answer if there were three buffalo?

Tomatoes, okra, and squash in the ground today. Even after the rain still clods; next year since the second year out of sod will be better.

I get the first *Salt Lick* in the mail tomorrow. Doing envelopes slowing me now, doing nice ones though. Some saved for a show of envelopes.

5-13-73

Waiting In Quincy

which to this one
is waiting like anywhere
has to be with itself

the day time
with my sympathies
for the facts   so making
mine   the day   all
would have

5-21-73

River up to 22 feet and now down again in this surely the end of the year's high water. W. Quincy still with 5 feet; the buildings slowly coming back.

The college let out, Randy & Dan graduated. Tomorrow I must get up and out to Payson High School to visit by 8:30. Well.

5-31-73*

A man of the middle lands. The land from this home

*First piece for projected "A Quincy History."

will be to the rest of the world. Each to the sun. How to live is our time, would there be a people in the flatland. I believe in all, it is my history.

———————

This as a starting place, a piece to return to. The form will probably be set in motion. Yes.

Lee returned by H&R. No one in mind now. The book is to be sat on now, *House* as companion with the ms.

Put peppers in the garden today, seven plants Tom Hillenbrand, new neighbor/old friend, gave me. Tomatoes, radishes doing well. Limas and bush beans making the way up. Good weather these next days will have them up.

6-1-73

This bay of the long river that some would call Boston Bay. It is here in the washes and on the bluff that the houses are built. Here we know the river divides, each bank. The water grown in spring greater than what we've known brings silt to balance the damage. Find a farmer who would sell his land flooded every three years, there are so few.

We live with the river and its waters.

7-3-73

First entry in a month. Finally settling in for the summer after being east to NYC, very fine visit with Gerald and Alessandra, Bob Taylor and Kathy Heinrich. Trammell & Ginger in Europe. Then D.C. Good to see Lee and Michael. Saw Johnny Winter. I graduated in Columbia, back to stake the tomatoes, a week in Texas with Dan Castelaz along.

7-20-73

Much work at the shop and at home though not much seeming to get done. Getting tomatoes, lettuce, and green beans out of the garden. First tomato very sweet and it looks as if I will be getting them for the rest of the summer.

Must get *South Orange Sonnets* review done and in the mail to *Granite,* but when. Greg Williams in town tomorrow night to fill in with Bluebirds. Sunday I drive to Pana for Mike Kennedy's wedding reception. Things begin to go smooth soon.

8-14-73

Rain the last week making things cooler than usual for this part of August. Pressed to finish a job contracted through the shop before Gerald's visit. —Both Gerald and Alessandra tired from the drive and ill. But by their fourth day had settled some. The visit much better with Gerald than with Alessandra, as I had to try to be polite after a while. The midwest and how things go from day to day a bit too much for her. They left, leaving a note since I was at a job with the band. Bo and Ellie Brown came in last night for a day to see the town and I helped to edit "Two Kids," a good piece and he will do better I believe.

So. My journal work tapered off through the summer as usual. Trying to humor a sore throat so I can make Mahavishnu this evening in Edwardsville.

Quincy House

if you build
here you must
build for yourself
the old money
keeping the other
out as they could

> if you would build
> business here you will
> not have your laborers
> come in   no   the people
> here are for the
> building

John Wood's cabin was the first, but for the last thousand Sauk; this was where they would end. Warriors of the north made to stand here. Old Sauk village.

8-21-73

People living where they will, the ones who from their closeness to a soil (middle western plains) are called without arts. Let it be craft. Since there is seldom time for it, a day to do everything. The issues being so much the same each day, there is a strength from it. Nothing leaves quickly, everything has time. The food situation now though. Really different than the one in New York City is still the same : the way items do last and don't.

I am holding things now I will finally give to others. What we use is that fit all tools make to us. There are simply more tool makers now. The music we

> can make is
> the music we

> this day to
> dance the music
> we can make
> is the music we
> can all dance to

This day to dance, the music we can make is the music we can make is the music we can all dance, to singing to one self.

8-25-73

Buried three cats today.

9-23-73

Very strong fumes from varnish on a piece of furniture in the kitchen. Putting it outside.

Getting a few of the chores out of the way from months back, the shop slowing as is its custom according to Bert. The times moving fast. Randy and Betty married the 15th in Alton. Dan staying here while he makes a place for himself downtown in the gallery. Framing envelopes for friends Schweda, Pierson, Dan.

In a letter Gerald figured upon the thing that has been at the core of my work halting, or the slowdown in my verse, not keeping journal. The summer and weather playing their usual part, but the distance furthered by not getting over the records, the string of facts for this place. I knew from the start that the journal would be true of me and turned to the books. But doing so, I lost sight of myself. No work to speak of, getting further from my intention's original.

My key to this is to return to the self sense after this reference. This history is to see. I want to see the books the shelves that stand them. A town would have books.

Few Minutes

> taking a yardstick
> which is already
> in here the kitchen
> a string through the
> nailhole and paper
> rolled to the end
> make a fine cat toy
> a thing for the small
> times this before bed

9-24-73

Bob Woodward and Frank Mankiewicz at the college this evening and good response from the town. Difficult to believe the platform and the public acceptance in regard to the sweeping changes in American political attitudes. No hostile reception even in questions afterward.

9-29-73

Rain.

Working well and getting past the cold I had. A full week ahead to pull more of the issue together; getting done though plenty more to do. But to get caught up to only envelopes would leave me fairly clear. Still getting tomatoes while the rest of the garden has passed.

a town not built
so much a town
to the river   believe

the nature of ours
streets either reaching
to the water or to
running with it
it is the same
for any paths near
the waters

things were built
living to the circle   breath in rock bluff
this place   there would   bottom oaks let
be books   the houses be blood
                             and there would
things I build   be books
living to the circle

breath   to   rock   bluff
bottom   oaks   let
the houses be   blood
and there would be
books

10-29-73

To begin so much happened since last time in the book
here.

Long talk with Dan one evening weeks ago where it was
decided that this present issue will be the last of *Salt Lick* as
consecutive magazine issue. Much harder than I thought.
It's not that I simply never thought of it as ending, but tim-
ing and the circumstances of Dan's feelings about it hard-
ened it. Just that if we were to work on, the time for the
magazine would be over; part of it his disappointment in
me, the magazine's success which excludes him (at least the
way most people see it). I recognize some of this as I'm
accountable, but I see most if it as direct difference of per-
sonality and how the magazine evolved. Not that I've ever
meant to deny the work he or Steve put in; but when someone writes, it's to me, or subscribes. Then people take for
granted everything in it as mine. I felt sad to see Dan feel
this way. Money issue used as well.—

Well, time for change. Honestly since that decision, I've
been lifted. Should finish up this issue by Christmas, then
put them on a shelf.

Finally got to piecing the poems of the last six months
together. Just seeing them as beginning, lead-in pieces, to the
history. Combined the two journal things as they were with
their swing into verse. Then the list reads:

lead-in   Still kicking with order
Sanctuary   though roughly chronological

Journal	excepting the first piece.
Roadside Artists	Also beginning to see this
W. Quincy Flood	and *House* as companions. Loose but
Waiting in Quincy	something to work with.
Real Estate	
Few Minutes	

Preoccupied with plans for the Halloween Costume Ball. Only Wednesday night and still much to do. But the bands make a little, we have a good time, pay all the bills, and hope to make enough so I can finish up this issue. Clean start next year. Texas for Christmas.

11-6-73

The Ball was a great party but failure as benefit. Went in the hole, but friends and creditors making it easier to pay the bills. So. Maybe easier next time, get this thing to run itself with hopes of making a grub stake for the press each year.

Getting the grant proposals done slowly, in the mail by the end of the week. First frost last night.

11-16-73

Williams' stand of words makes one think of it as correct just as everything else I've heard. "Writing made of words . . ." it would seem indisputable; Silliman's vocal opposition to the statement carrying less the weight he intended since there is room for both of their works in the words, and perhaps it's just that Silliman would have liked to have said it first. All is tied to itself in language.

Today there is a poetry in Syllable and it is seen as sophisticated to experiment in phrase, line, object-referentiality letting the page climate dictate meaning as well as audience. But if a language is alive, it has as many possibilities as those who use it can imagine. A language of one, so much the world exists between your word day and mine.

From the news, I gather that a poet tied to realizing and growing a personal vocabulary is turning away from all the possibilities of the universe save one. But it seems to be me. Simply, each day all is more. What is love tomorrow? A poetry that would speak to each one just as the rain falling on any head and the grass. Perhaps it's general as opposed to specific language though seldom consistently so. Bill Schneider mentioned a place between realizing the specific and universal, no doubt poems from that place. But is a house built there. Perhaps. Things go on there.

12-4-73

Back from a week away. First stop in Peoria overnight with Dick; met Al Moritz there visiting a friend of his, Mike Foster. Al very much taken with Gerald's work; a very positive review in the new *Shore Review* of *BM.* Had a chance to thank him in person. Then to Chicago to visit with the Castelazes; Dan and Kieren announcing their engagement. Very happy for them, looks good.

Rest of the week with Barbara on the north side. Good visit, also saw Dan McD, Bo & Ellie Brown. Sore throat slowed this a bit at the last. Worked on an article with Curt Johnson and met Jack Conroy at the bus late one night. Great man Conroy, great energy.

Citizen

> less the land that begins the air
> as mountains where they are various
> to the soil   an ocean   any pool the
> living common   a brightest morning
> marks the century

1-3-74

First entry for a new year. Busy through the last month with little time to myself, but a fine holiday.

To start, went to Muscatine, Iowa with the band the night before I planned to leave for the southwest. Caught in the first sizable snow of the season which stranded us overnight in Rock Island with Angie & Judy Varias. The next day spent driving the 160 or so miles just to get back to Quincy. Waited two days before starting again; overnight in Joplin with Sherrie & George, getting to Dallas on Christmas Eve. All in all the best Christmas I can remember.

The trip back ok to Joplin, but then caught in the second big storm of the year. Eleven hours to drive in from Joplin, snow all the way. One lane traffic. Now a day or two after and the house working again, food, clean, car frozen.

No time in Texas to work on that piece for *Southwest Review,* but did think a few things through for it. Aided by the lines in some 50s musical about a fashion magazine editor. In their plot building, the writers evidently felt that defining the role of their magazine was necessary and things they defined come close to fitting any periodical. But perhaps I can get a draft down.—

Oh, also a show {painted envelopes} in Geneva, Switzerland to get things into by Feb. 14.

1-15-74

Seems more and more I'm losing readers. People who find these poems of the history, and *House* to an extent, to be less than earlier poems. This disappoints. Slater rejection of *A Quincy History* was not exactly a total surprise, but depressing. And his saying that he couldn't read some of them; but I know people can't read people sometimes. Burns letter just received. Fuel for his arguments that I haven't enough company that would survive if literary principles enforced. This isn't coming straight. Just hard finding myself more removed than I realized.

1-16-74

A magazine will come into a home. Because of that it has to add. The movement of magazines in any manner is response to a demand, a personal demand. It's the difference of people that shows how some are pushed while others stroll to that end. A true magazine will assume its material, adopted complexion to suit it, wearing heart to page.

There was a magazine that did not ride in a car and for that reason there are now cars and more. Moving one thing to another with a hand to the paper, in the instance preferring print, consider an almanac by nature as teaching the one who would take it up; and understanding that one, an almanac chose to listen to all it heard. Corn into bushels to understand the field, livestock from the hand to another, diseases and their fare taking positions in order to understand a people to their land and air. An almanac can be a better magazine.

1-22-74

Sudden chronicles for a lifespan. It's a matter of gathering the things important in a less important way. Reasons show themselves more quickly here and so they appeal to an audience in like character, and displease also.

I mostly end up giving the boxes that fill with periodicals to the town school libraries so readers have choice in the matter, any time down to that believing what you know and what is read. A good one both.

New places always close behind, a magazine would be a pamphlet, a handbill, the cave drawings paper, and the moons, not the star. The stars.

1-23-74

Love of others, love of beasts, love of cookery and the house.

1-30-74

The ever widening local set and grown in all what a day would bring. Centeredness the gift in the acts, begin instances begin events. It was only a matter of time before records of event became decorative; and this to forgive magazines. It shows itself meeting its normal appetites, where what makes it must speak to more, and does given someone sees it. In dim light, begin to see all things leaning to themselves.

> any move it makes
> that is noticed   hear
> all this house talk
> simple wood come iron
> common glass every inch
> a breath

2-14-74

Every bit, each part, this part, how many. All the times I would embrace this.

It is more than reading Whitman lately, though seeing him now as if never before. Castelaz says how else can it be for our education that I see any American writer taking a place toward Whitman from necessity. More than the inheritance in language, his placement of poetry in society and how the poet (". . . the greatest poet . . ." and ". . . the greatest poem . . .") takes place, there point generations. Finding myself believing so in a parallel to him and knowing that it is from him and yet believing that my individual discovery is the essence of his work, while giving strength to my voice. The most obvious question: what left to write; and obvious answer: everything. Perhaps of this unsettlement comes a sense of loss, losing the notion that it was secretly (my secret) important that I provide the work I felt given to in order to explain things, make it easier on someone. How am I surprised it is me.

3-5-74

SMALL PIECES FOR GLOBAL SYMPHONY

Living on a corner of less than busy streets in the middle of a small town, traffic sounds are common enough, though the birds wake me this morning. For the most part sparrows, jays, and given mourning doves, and it is so today. The dying elms in front of the house themselves sound in the considerable wind last few days, clicking. A storm will usually bring a large branch down, Dutch Elm Disease and no known cure.

The low hum of the factories that hold east and then west on the river would be the louder, if nothing else were. River traffic barges long horn, lasting almost a minute. Mississippi.

Someone in the neighborhood using a hammer. At random, most every day.

James Haining
Quincy, Illinois

For Mieko Shiomi
Sakaguchi 1-24-38
Sakura, Minoo
Osaka, Japan

5-26-74

First entry in many weeks. Very much happened, just to set some of it here and take up journal again.

Show in Peoria good. A solid week of framing, hanging, lectured on magazine at a fine arts festival at Illinois Central

College; Philip José Farmer also there. Cold set in after travel, etc. that had me down a while, but in good health and spirits.

Rain. Rain. Not as much as last year, but seems the same. Half the garden in, but so much rain since I've not had a chance to put in the rest. Lettuce, tomatoes, peppers, and onions in. Beautiful green town.

School out, finished seminar with a look at the more recent good ones, and it went well. Seems little chance that I will teach there, little money, and none for curriculum. Ridge the new chairman.

Playing much lately. Plans for taping this 4th. Scattered report. Moving vaguely toward something. More. The summer before me.

MAGAZINE

A magazine will come into a home. Because of that it has to add. It's the difference of people that shows how some are pushed while others stroll to that end. A true magazine will assume its material, adopted complexion to suit it, wearing heart to page. ❧ There was a magazine that did not ride a car and for that reason there are now cars and more. Moving one thing to another with a hand to the paper, in the instance prefering print, consider an almanac by nature as teaching the one who would take it up; and understanding that one, an almanac chose to listen to all it heard. Corn into bushels to understand the field, livestock from the hand to another, diseases and their fare taking places in order, to a people to their space. An almanac can be a better magazine. ❧ Sudden chronicles for a lifespan. It's a matter of gathering the things important in a less important way. Reasons show themselves more quickly here, and so they appeal to an audience in like character, and displease also. I mostly end up giving the boxes that fill with them to the town school libraries so readers have choice in the matter, anytime down to that believing what is known, what is read. A good one both. ❧ New places always colse behind, a magazine would be a pamphlet, a handbill, the cave drawings paper, and the moons, not the star. The stars. ❧ Love of others, love of beasts, love of cookery and the house. ❧ The ever widening local, set and grown in all what a day would bring. Centeredness the gift in the acts, begin instances begin events. It was only a matter of time before records of event became decorative; and this to forgive magazines. It shows itself meeting its normal appetites, where what makes it must speak to more, and does given someone sees it. In dim light, begin to see all things leaning to themselves.

> any move it makes
> that is noticed   hear
> all this house talk
> simple wood come iron
> common glass every inch
> a breath

> James Haining
> —from *A QUINCY HISTORY*

Printed page for *Happiness Holding Tank* of mag piece. Only one typo, but I guess that makes it authentic.

5-31-74

Jaspe Days

> traveling case
> of my books
> it began as a
> sample kit
> for a Moorman's Man
> fertilizer I think
> and divided calcium
> next to lime rows
> soil samples   but

the books all
have the musk
it gives   as
you open it

Worst storm of the year. Tornado hits Ursa, several houses destroyed. Trees here turned up, lines down in our yard. Circles and coils charred in the wet ground. Linemen all over town with power out; finally did ours at 1:30 in the morning. Flash floods south of us, all the nearby rivers out of their banks at points. Salt, Illinois, Mississippi, and Fabius.

6-6-74

Reading with candle McMurtrie's "The Book" while the electricity is out. Another storm tonight. Digging through the first few chapters on the history of prehistoric writing, and just up to the origins of the alphabet. Amazing how the Greeks took things piecemeal to come up with the relative I use here. He gives them credit for setting a standard left to right order for writing, setting Phoenician characters aside for special duty and thus the first vowels, diphthongs, and a few others. —Funny tie up. Greeks before setting the order standard left/right, used it as well as the older Phoenician right/left, and a peculiar alternate form (l/r, r/l, l/r) called boustrophedon, "ox-turn-like."

Finally getting the rest of the garden in the other day with Ray, it occurred while stringing twine for even rows that the practice must have born out of utilitarian purposes, even rows allowing more food per space. The pleasing sight of even rowed fields a matter of beauty long before the plow, pleasing in what the fields hold against the harvest. The alphabet in earliest forms used by tradesmen rather than the Egyptian or Babylonian characters since it was more *useful.* To the point. They think it traces to the Sinai mining outposts Egyptians set up with local foremen; the clerks teaching the natives rudiments of writing as a lark, the locals transcending them. —If the language in spite of given education really comes of the place, then only natural that my verse is so here. Not as simple as middlewestern flat, even Gerald using that handle now and again; but more the energy of association I was given to calling sound earlier. Sound as I *understand* it my first tip-in for sure, but I am coming in around that now. Real *use* of the words now, use the words, mean as they can. No wonder people won't read the work since *House;* different dialectic. I begin to see my work coming out of the day in a way never before. So simple if I let it.

6-17-74

Letter the other day from Gerald that I just got around to answering this evening. Inside tonight after a long day, six hours at Doc's. But Gerald not liking "Jaspe" poem and a line I had made about not feeling much to it, the weight of History inclusion. Well. He bit it directly. My being spooked at my own work, trying to write a poem after the magazine piece and consciously not let it affect, and of course it did. Felt foolish at forgetting the few things I believe learned thus far in the long book. So it's to make all the work the book, then I can forget the book; Gerald and letters so generous, ok. Poems as they will. The book, book hand to heart.

I mean his vision of me, though only part; its touch is to the center.

7-10-74

Well. Beginning to come to senses from the holiday. So many people here at the house; many of the old people back in town, a good 4th at Doc's. The women back to visit their own source of pleasure; Barb and Ginger here at the house. Funny way getting closer to Barbara all the time. . . . . Heat

wave and doing lots of work hard to come back to journal
though. Talk. Many letters from Gerald and some of my
energies there, but uncomfortable with myself. Old excuse
of summer months where little seems to move head, time
less conscious with spirit, should say brain.

Thinking of new History work, but shy to it. John
Woods and his walking. Still reading McMurtrie's book and
new one sent from Gerald by Fussell: *Lucifer in Harness.*
Looks fine in first few pages. Michael writes to send a book
of my poems to Some Of Us Press since they are looking at
things from people outside of DC. Not *A Quincy History* but
earlier things, haven't looked yet, but waiting. Seven readers
to pass through, so only fair chance. Perhaps read it tonight.

Jaspe Days

traveling case
of my books
sample kit
for a Moorman's
Man I think
and divided
fertilizer—calcium
line rows soil
samples musk books
it gives it opening it

Siren For Boy

his same voice
to first answer
it then
as he chooses
to hear it

    his own
    playing new
    swing set

Curious time between poems. That is my life recent days. Soon when I've filled the ravine at Spring Lake, I will start binding with the old man.

10-16-74

Heartland's Furrow

    other pieces in binding
    word joists a house
    pieces for world judgement

    more than a   lover a
    word softly Barbara
    moves the room   some

    small musics

Long absence from journal. Since then the rapid end of summer and fall, now getting cold. Toward winter. Let's see, I was in Chicago for Dan & Kieran's wedding late in July. Then in Texas for two weeks; except for a day, spent the time in Whitney. Back home here, busy with the band and work. A finished application in for an NEA grant for the books took weeks; I'm getting worse at forms. Now working daily at the shop, running the press at times, but mostly doing artwork and camera set up.

Garden almost gone, just a few tomatoes left. A good one this year, though neglected through the middle of the summer, when everyone gone. In two days, I leave for California. Driving a truck of antiques and Suzy Irwin to her house in Mill Valley. Looking ahead to the trip, change of scenery. Never got that west before.

An entry today just to get back. Cold in the kitchen, will turn on the heat after I'm back. Two weeks. Winter and the books tomorrow.

11-24-74
Mill Valley

Second day here. Took five in crossing with the truck. Feel good today with rest; the trip taking its toll.

First chance to take in the desert in length, beautiful things. The mountains in New Mexico a surprise. Spent the night in Tucumcari, then to the Grand Canyon. Stayed at a lodge on the south rim, next morning took the canyon in. Everything I expected and more, thus a desire to return. Moved around to the western rim, Bright Angel. Stopped again in Barstow, California. High desert. Through the mountains and valleys, smog more than apparent 120 miles from L.A., up the central valley to the Bay area. Too tired to see much going through S.F. the night we arrived, so will see today. Almost beautiful enough to overcome my sense of disbelief. It's the same feeling I got in Georgetown, and other places seemingly occupied with willful suspension of disbelief. Paradise and only two miles from the freeway.

Brought one book with me, *Maximus.* I listen to Alice Coltrane, thinking about a wind piece for that collection in Japan. Will most likely be the truck and its movements.

11-4-74

Back a week tomorrow. Several days in just getting my rest. I flew to Texas for two days, mainly to see Grandaddy who is slowly coming to his end. He was glad to see me as was Nanny who looks better than she has. Seems when one ill the other, having to be strong, truly rises in the moment. He tells me I probably won't see him alive again; he also tells me to sit up in my chair. Guess John Watson was one of the considerable influences in my life. A good man.

Busy in the house, so cold tonight. No heat save the oven in the kitchen here. Will have the furnace primed for the winter tomorrow. Also talk to Ridge about teaching at the college. Don't expect much to come of it, save hopefully I'll stop thinking about it for a time.

Gerald getting stronger in Michigan; I'm letters behind. Michael in Spain. Will most likely be in Chicago this weekend for Rich Lutz's wedding, then settle down for a time. Be still. Come back to journal.—

Two men in the tavern talking about roses. When how far down to cut them back. One of them especially taken with the "Peace rose"; white with red mingled down in it.

11-5-74

Finally decided I like "Jaspe Days" after being down on it, most likely because Gerald didn't like it. Said I couldn't write a poem about the smell my books get. Just read the poem and saw it there. Then new one.

Heart In Senses

> just as frequent seems
> two men sitting
> in the tavern   not
> Calf Town but
> north side
>
> there talking to how
> and when roses to
> be cut back

Title possibly change, no won't.
Heat turned on and feels good. Strong day, lots done.

Michael back from Europe. Tomorrow I'll call and compare notes on finalized ms. His, Gerald's, and my list of exclusions. Earliest work in the first section of the book getting the most attention, second best left to *South Orange Sonnets* as Gerald said early on, and last section almost complete as Michael sends. And I'm more toward getting the early than either. The work turning back into itself so many times, each time in a different way. All Michael's. Just peeling back. So maybe the book done shortly; then have two and more push to find the solution to the composition problem. Some printer's devil.

Listening just now before bed to Robert Petway. And early Fenton Robinson. Radio show tomorrow.

11-6-74

Resting. Into November and today took tomatoes from the garden—so late into the season. Only matter of days I believe until the freeze that will end the garden. A generous thing the garden and even so in neglect. From a time of initial care in cultivating and planting, care is not unduly. How am I amazed with it over again? Garden out the window, last squash too hard to eat in the weeds and now leaves. Still tomatoes. Carrots confused with the grass, green peppers still standing too. I won't pull the poles until everything brown.

How beneficial the human among the plants. I begin to wonder at the city and its people imposed to place. Many still frightened of the forest. But I must not understand the large cities. Yes, they generate their own. Perhaps, of each place, inbreeding through the ages finally sympathetic.

Olson the only book I took west, and I knew I wouldn't read much, but my copy of *Max* anyway. Opened at random, brilliant Charlie moving down the page. Never quite read like this before, coming across much faster and better than the first few times. Seems a familiarity brewed in my,

its, absence. Expect to take more in. Beautiful #6, and
Bright Angel no less.

> Build this house
> John Wood town
> many before the
> octagon mansion
> just as apples
> not yielding at first
> and walked to Alton
> for the pint   three
> seed produce trees
>
> an orchard reinvents
> itself
>   and need
> flowers

11-14-74

Day after the first snow. Slack work at the shop, thus
open afternoons. Don and Cal from the radio station over
for supper. Oil my shoes this evening against the weather.

Gerald sends page six of the new book: a human poem,
more vulnerable therein than Gerald usually allows. Not allow, wrong word, just that the place is more direct from
experience rather than reflection. The place the poem
dwells is that place where lover would plea, realize, seeing
that love through. His settling A in his soul. Gerald (his
verse) more human than first impressions generally allow,
the obvious intimidation in the presence of such thinking.
Works the last ten months moving progressively from the
protection I think he sometimes sought in the earlier ones
(*BM*), more to the open. Physically this would parallel with
his attentions to his McC and enduring the end of the mar-
riage. Fleeing NYC. I see this as good, and suffer in my small

ways for him. Encourage the move. Now he's talking of
going back to Texas perhaps. Or staying in the north woods.

> mink oiled all leather
> shoes   boots   shop shoes
> that are garden shoes
> speckled paint slippers
> finally supple evening
> more shoes than a grandfather
> might have but worn to
> to an end as he

11-17-74

For Mieko Shiomi
SPATIAL POEM NO. 8
  WIND EVENT – October 7-27, 1974

> Given air wind poem.
> Most general senses of
> Room, wind in moment.
> Duration is destination.

During the time, I drove a five ton box truck
roughly 2,400 miles beginning in Quincy, Illinois and
concluding in Mill Valley, California. The cargo of
this vehicle aside from myself and Suzy Irwin being
Indian rugs, paintings, china, and furniture. Five
days.

> South Rim Grand Canyon
> Bright Angel
> warms   to   floor

Sequential wind. That there are six of the seven
climate changes to floor of the canyon. Airs. As
much generating themselves, each and other. Imagine canyon as device, matter device. A wind here

will to Missouri and beyond, each mile the next fol-
lows to an end.

> each day in breathing
> wind dance

> from work one works
> children to ideas winded

12-1-74
1–2 AM

Seven inches of snow and just turning December. The
rotting tomatoes left in the garden, a grand tan color, are
soft curves in the snow tonight. So much this early snow
gives the local and St. Louis predictions of the worst winter
in a hundred years weight. Seemed silly when I heard them
saying the wooly worms were the wrong color, black rather
than brown, which was a strong sign; but I remember seeing
them crossing the highways through Missouri and Oklahoma while driving west. A hard time won't help anyone, because the country is already staggering. It seems to be repeating itself: the harsh consequences of our own deeds
tallied with equally severe response from environment. The
trouble in the world generating into the earth, then returned
in kind. The doom-peddlers are particularly busy, but most
everyone is thinking. My mother, grandparents, predicting
this for years, though mother recently worrying to me. Can't
help but be glad they are out of the city and living there in
the hill country.

My work to breathe new. New strides to it, as I learn to
see past the first accomplishments of it which have comfort-
ed me. Time to push off this. A letter from Gerald helping to
define a like feeling whose direction I was unsure of. Large
concerns once again looming in the distance. Weight in *A
Quincy History* one, a thing I also had to settle in finishing
the work on Michael's book. The easy part being the elimi-

nation of work that actually would eliminate itself through repetition, repeating itself to no good purpose. This process time consuming, though not as difficult as the part to follow. Since so much of the work is autobiographical, it was a matter of condensing which allows the ms. to assume its natural density and texture without distortion. The hard part being the elimination of work that more recently written would force itself on the body of the rest of the material. Not simply a change in stream, though intentions would be that of the ms. itself and revelations excluded from any of the work so far, but a move toward self-direction that I sense self-defeating. Michael felt a particular affection for the piece "My Life" which in senses was indicative of his actions. Saying things as an act of faith for the first time in his poetry like starting a new relationship with someone and not needing to lie. All this tension robs the verse though where in stride his genius at defeating time consequences. His work is that. I begin to feel sensations that this is also where I stood in defending "Jaspe Days" with Gerald. Defense from a self-defeating place. Just hard to listen.

12-14-74
2-12-75

Two months. Last rushed days before the holiday left me to the *Lucky Heart* flyers; Bill Harris and Bill Browner both here the last two days before the trip to Texas; 22nd I think. Also happy to wake up the day of the drive and find my cold gone; spent a quiet time home, solid Christmas. Dennis still not quite his usual self which to me was sensitive, but gaining confidence. —Rested mostly. My last two days were full though; spent Saturday in Dallas to see grandparents, then saw David and Bob. Great time! Hadn't seen either for a long while, Bob for years. While Bob is writing constantly, David is writing less and less. Trammell must have shown me six consecutive volumes of *George*

Washington Trammell. Saw the boxed set of pieces on individual pages, can't think of the name unless *Cenotaph.* Told him it would make a great combined edition: build boxes with David Searcy prints/Burns drawings. Also a book about three cars Trammell wrecked. Still wonderful people to know. —Sunday was a full day in Whitney with the burial of Addie Treadaway, oldest of her branch. It was the first occasion in a long time to pull relatives together from all three families: really Simons and Treadaways and the Watsons who are directly connected. Rained, but let up. Rained all the way to an hour before Quincy. Stayed five hours overnight with Sherrie and George. Then more rest.

2-19-75

Hadn't been back for more than a few weeks when Ray and Randy and I bought an addressing and mailing business. We moved the equipment from the garage in Calf Town where the young wife operated it, to an empty apartment in the Lahl's building. There it sits; business in town and nation slow. Hell of a time to go into business, but what else? We have jobs coming up in April and June; all of us also trying to sell. We try it. —Also worked out an idea hit upon while with my brothers in Texas. It's a sampler. Small book to fit in pocket with selections from the books that will follow it in the *Lucky Heart* series. Only days after my birthday, I was lucky to find typesetting here at $8 an hour which revived my work on the books. Decided to try the samplers idea, used my work to experiment with in case of failure, but happily it turned well. It is a 5½" × 6" folded and stapled pamphlet; contains only poems since *House,* using "Lifetime," "Journal," "Sanctuary," "Roadside Artists," "Waiting In Quincy," "W. Quincy Flood," "Few Minutes," "Siren For Boy," and "Heart In Senses." Printed it all, and not too bad a job. I did it without Bert helping me, in fact worked mostly on a weekend as no one was there. Finished the assembly Monday morning and counted 450. My little book.

So with luck I will have all the books set and printed by summer, then turn to binding. Expect to do some study in technique and perhaps build some of the equipment.

Gerald living in Uniondale and sounding better. His divorce may be final early in March, but he is deeply in love with McC. He sent a letter recently that was morbid in his sense of approaching death; tried to shake that in reply, and see it as passing. He seems to be perking up. Just got a copy of "Hermetic Journal" but have had no time really to read. Will.

Going to Tom Hillenbrand's seminar; good to be reading some. Reading verse somewhat, what's new to the library shelves: Bly's last one typical of him—to no improvement I think/also some Cid Corman *Living/Dying* which in places shines. At times he considers sound the way I do, or did maybe two years ago. Like some of his things only.

2-24-75

Made most of a first mailing of the sampler today: the work of addressing and letters to all subscribers and friends woven in with the sudden winter storm that has sixteen inches official snowfall on the town and more tonight. Everyone digging out, not really. Only ones young or needing to move. Some yards placid and without dogs secure in the snow. But a good letter from Gerald receiving sampler. His excitement also with a new ms. that he sees intended for sampler format, *Nations in Public.* A dialog of the character in the nationals he is drawn from: Scot, Irish, Polish. This is discounted in last paragraph where he would have the work aimed differently; he in letter saying he had no plans for the thing except as a possible (partly) bio thing for an anthology, until samplers came. But I agree it would make a fine piece for a sampler; the *Letters* not fitting unless picked for size, and "Hermetic Journal" not suited easily. So. May get to work on it this week. Write him tomorrow.

3-6-75

Tomorrow I pick the finished *Nations in Public* set finally in Bodoni, letting Baskerville go for the moment. May begin printing it this weekend. Anxious to get to it. May need to do an additional printing of the *AQH* one, too, as I'm almost out.

Nice card today from Bruce Andrews. He found himself surprised with the sampler, glad he can read it.

4-3-75

Spent a day at the shop to run first leaves of *NP*. Half the day spent cleaning the shop. Spring mood, then snow tonight.

Another bit for poem today, set it all now in the book. Perhaps call it Pangaean.

        all porcelain dishes better
        bowls whose light extended
        in curve   would schools
        be so   a spectrum lives
        in its origins without water
        or classroom windows hosting
        common glass will

        womens hands how
        else a totem magic near
        the river   considered
        death of animals on the islands
        in high water gone there low
        through the heat
        painted spots but finger prints
        our primitive meaning by each moment

old Sauk village   dogged here
by the Northern tribes   last place
there last energy to hold
lest they see the camp burn

best painters hunt bison
in the rock before the hand
to ocher   natural hole   for eye
swollen back in clay   animal
lying on animal found image
very soon   space

ones love
for this north american plate
in the absence of alps
folded high new earth
below old   none the less so
for Pangaea   whose rift
marks turn in touch the
given peoples

shelves brined
half an inch centuries
to limestone   its food
internal a garden
of plants rock makers
lifted from seas floor
to cliff top

mantle

always   once alive

3-20-75
Busy at the shop to the point of not being able to finish

Gerald's *Nations in Public* as I choose. Perhaps tomorrow. No index [stock] for the covers till it comes, so must wait. Running the press more and more and looking forward to the books. First spring days yesterday and today. Have a third of the garden turned and my back yielding to it; may get the rest this weekend, work to do at the office tho. All things moving with the new days. Verse absent for the time, but I think of the poem entered last; think in terms of its concern—at once removed but founded commonness. Small terms of insects and life in the water, be here as unlike elsewhere, but seen in kind. Seeing in kind, what this book would, it goes no easier for given difficult. Its own example.

The cat sleeping with my shoes, the ones I wear in the garden. Not the soil, but I wear them, and they fit well.

3-24-75

Finished the first of Gerald's samplers today. Got a few in the mail to him, but almost all of them to finish at the shop. So get them done, to the books. I may find it more difficult to do them than I previously thought. Just my uncertainty as to the binding. So.

> veined milk skin
> breasts the girl
> has breakfast listening
> the farmer is important
> his plans   as
> April

4-7-75

A dun sky how better here, or any the town beneath it.

4-16-75

Much happened in passing. Bob Trammell and Deborah Riddles here overnight on their way to Milwaukee for a verse conference. Snyder the main draw, as well as Nathaniel Tarn and J. Rothenberg. But so good to see Bob; the most time we've spent together in three years. He always amazes, and pretty Deborah who has presence; no easy feat while Bob and I go crazy. Made tentative plans for his sampler, *Dog* the concept/to go with Dog Show he plans for fall in Dallas . . . from the sound and looks of it, the arts festival the two of them pulled together in Dallas was a huge success. Over two hundred participants. Maybe another in the fall, and I may do a reading.

So busy and now four jobs. Don't seem to make progress in any direction but the days. Thinking almost daily about the *History.* In senses learning the lesson of love for place. That I would hold this small town and its own so closely, but not to lose myself to it. What I would know of the others by this life; I begin to learn my poetry.

5-2-75

That it would be, as after things. How else to address the surviving, the facts around the noticed, whose best art is not declared because it fills the days. Naming will not be enough, unless it defines. Rough river's bluff given way to rolled hills, to talk about, while the people get their wagons over. Still getting the wheels over this day, and grace always as considered. History the way of seeing such graces, them all. Our country that continues in subject, not narrator. But history would begin to speak after. We would call it that.

5-19-75

The window for the kitchen on the house across the yard is crooked. Just less than the upright, but opens. A half window; easily held, and harder to square. The house being built, the windows lying near the barrow no less perfect. Turning from the board, not afraid to touch this.

bended to weeds
in the garden
one hand to a
valise   a printer home
from shop just walked there
with the cats mulberries
all over it down
from the wind there not in
time time to see

6-17-75

Busy times, but come back to journal. I am being forced to spend more of my time working for a wage now. Making a place for myself at the shop; Bert somewhat reluctantly conceding failures in the business, but that a good sign. Also the newspaper, *Mississippi Star,* getting on. I printed the first issue this week. Had to fight it every inch: trying to run against the grain a sheet that barely fit the press limits. First time I ever ran a job that large. I will improve; and if the paper becomes as regular as expected, my study of the press will accelerate. Ink on my hands. My glasses. Feet won't wash white from the mulberries underfoot in the garden. What I've been doing.

6-22-75

Met Luther Allison at the Swan Dive in Canton, Illinois last Monday night. Did a piece for the *Star,* not too bad. Just trying to understand my disappointment with his music, while appreciating his strength. So, I learn a little. And get back into work for Salt Lick Press. Mailed 700 pieces for the *Lucky Heart* books, so further committed to their completion. Grant money here soon. With Gerald's ms. gone, I am a little at a loss as to getting rolling again. A good stroke of luck, the ms. return, would be most welcome.

Squash

young plants
before flower or
yellow crook necks
I water   water is
loud on the leaves
maybe six or less
leaves on them so
early vines just
started up

7-7-75

The day after last entry, a card came from Gerald saying the ms. of *Letters* finally arrived in Michigan. So, the luck. Also an invitation to be a literature consultant for Illinois Arts Council, one year, no salary. Late night call from Mother saying Margarete had died. I still haven't quite realized it. Made the quick drive which took 15 hours and helped with the funeral. Jack took it hard, malpractice suit possible. I took a virus and was a day late in leaving, then car trouble in Pryor, Oklahoma. Still ill. No help from local mechanics; they had the pickup towed to me, switched cars and drove on to Illinois. A week since 4th celebration and many friends in town. Great time at Doc's in Missouri.

Strange to say and begin unsure, but I have had the strongest pull from Texas after this last trip since we moved here. I know the emotion of the death and consequent gathering of family is still strong, but that doesn't explain all that I feel. I begin to want to move. This confuses me: after all *A Quincy History,* and such friends and the river. But it is a fresh pulse, and a weight lifted. Don't have plans, but am willing once more, figuring a year to tie loose ends and pay on school bills. Perhaps travel, though the country is in a subtle tailspin. Industrially impossible, politically improbable. Sparrows boil over the last bread heels on the porch. I wait for the garden food, green beans in days. One tomato. Onions.

Turn July

took them for
the party   about
six green onions
tied them white
folded ribbon next
to bulb and roots
untrimmed four
children in the
water   went out to
throw buckets of
at them   my little
to the big cool down

7-10-75

First letter from Gerald in some time. His surprise at my talk of a move. He tries to get hired, and an odd twist of the time has a writing instructor in Dallas a most recent suicide. May find Gerald in replacement. All I want to do now is realize these books. Getting close in spite of disappointment at how long I've been bogged down on the same. Friend looking for used equipment in St. Louis. Think to try Peoria. Parents here soon. Two days now cooler weather, catch up on some work.

7-27-75

Worked long days at the shop the past few weeks, 60 plus hours, and moving on the eventual completion of *Salt Lick* too. Can see the end of them—all fruits pages done, another 175 or so covers to do before the final assembly.

Then a little to do on remaining portfolios, and finally envelopes. All this can be done before the end of August, and shall be. Hard, and in ways possibly silly to stick to this since it as well as books having hung in the air, how many journal entries, moaning to complete. But it is almost like training now. The shop work is building up my duration and second wind, hopefully I can get a break soon and will have shape to move on it. Look to fall, one more month of summer.

Go to Chicago in three days. Anxious to see Dan and friends. Supposed to meet Eileen Shukofsky. Try to see some used equipment at Tompkins. Maybe some blues. Dan asks if I want to see Mexico and some Central America in August, but no time or $. I will try and talk him into waiting until January. I could use the new scenery. Think about school in another year. —New book by Kip Zeegers, *Back Yard.* Good collection, he will be a good one. Just wish he would loosen.

> Yellow the second color of the garden.
> Large squash flowers the brightest,
> darker than mustard, but a hard
> gold next to the tomatoes flowering.
> Pollen as well. Okra blossoms at the
> front of the plot, almost cousin to
> dogwood, only yellow to a purple
> center where dogwood white into magenta.
> The petals withered to a cap on the
> young okra pod, goes up. Starts up
> the same with the crook necks until the turning,
> their name, and the squash skin beads.
> Came in the house after tying
> the tomatoes again, and my hands soaped
> a bright yellow in the sink.

8-6-75

DISAPPEARING EVENT

June 2–July 22
Spatial Poem No. 9

Passage, in senses duty. A space
left by that love would move.
To leave place, by the love, travels
under more sky, at disappearing
embrace by the river.

moving three saucers
closer to each other
for what it has done
the sill
        three plants
taking the light for
the window

For Mieko Shiomi
Sakaguchi 1–24–38
Sakura, Minoo
Osaka, Japan

8-22-75

So much since the last journal, just run it down. The
trip to Chicago was interesting, perhaps learned a bit. Finally getting a Salt Lick Press account set up and using it. Fine
visit with Castelaz and spent an evening with Barbara, first
time in a year. Then my family finally came. Lots of fun, but
only here for a little more than two days. First visit by them
all since I left home. Gary and Dennis grown so much.
Mother loved the house and all; Poppa seeming to enjoy the
visit though uneasy about leaving the business, so the departure Sunday morning. Geoff Himes, Dan McDonell and

Diahn Miller here a week later and just left the day before yesterday. Nice visit. Always nice. Talked a little about schools as I begin to look into graduate schools. Sort of brought on in Chicago while talking with Anania. He mentioned Hopkins, Brown, and then offers an assistantship to Circle Campus there, if I'm interested. Chicago my last choice, Hopkins a strong second behind Brown. There is apparently a three year Dr. of Arts at Providence that looks to be the best program I might find; the rest are one year MFA in creative writing. Boston U. another one, maybe U. of N.H. Funny that I hadn't thought of school for so long, then the idea and now I would go. Don't know where, but it seems the best thing from all the different considerations. Will be four years absent by the time I go back. But there is no one I want to study under; I know I will learn wherever. Figure if I can muster an assistantship, I'd be foolish not to take it as I now see the chance of a school situation favorably. More access to tools, ideas. Gives a year to sell the business, finish books, clean out accounts. See the move as good; suppose I knew that before I would let myself talk about it. Parents reluctantly agree with my logic, friends supportive. The ten year *A Quincy History* not over, just moves. I have much to do.

8-29-75

Printed all by one sheet and covers each for Michael's sampler and second printing *A Quincy History*. Tomorrow Bo Brown's longer one, some collating. Mike Theys to help; with Bert out of town and his work caught up, I want to get all of my work done. With the Labor Day holiday, I can use the place Monday too.

9-25-75

When I almost finished everything on those new samplers, again visitors. Ginger and two women back on their way to NYC after the Naropa session over. Zheyna and Aziza, beautiful visit. Little sleep in working and being with them. Had found myself meeting a new circle of people here through Kathy Fritzmeyer. Then Michalea Moore. A poet, and we see each other. My luck and an eye infection that got suddenly worse the afternoon Gerald left; he arrived on a drive from Michigan to Texas, 2:30 in the morning, leaving at 3:30 in the afternoon. So good to talk with him. I laid a pallet on the floor for him. He is thinner, but I believe getting stronger. Stopped in Columbia after he left, according to the letter just from Texas. There is a painting he gave me on the wall of this bedroom. It is between the two windows. Four bathers by a lake, the one in Michigan surely. He accepted a painted envelope, to keep paper in—what else. Yesterday got a postcard from Robert Bly who was taken with the barn sampler; I'm just forwarding it to Bo, his surprise. Both he and Michael pleased. Typos in both, but aim for clean books.

9-28-75

Eyes still not back. A woman backs into the car; my new job. I worked three days last week, got a check. Not bad, learning to use paper running plates, new camera. Better wage, and it is full time.

So, just beginning to reorder the works, time for books, everything. Bert not liking my leaving, but resolved. I may still do the Lucky Heart books there. At present preferring metal to paper masters, but want to try these new ones a while longer. Good printing if the original is quality; the books would be. Set upstairs. Weather turns, cold inside. Holds it in the day, sometimes warmer outside. Open the windows.

10-19-75

A quiet, sunny day. Warm. Two new space heaters in

the front room to be installed sometime this week. Looks like it will be warmer this winter. Strange, the motion all these changes, is taking, takes together. New job a little less new, getting a steady income and learning to use it; even thinking of selling some furniture to pay off some bills. Seeing Michalea often, nice. Find the weeks go quickly, especially the workday. Get off at 4:30 and check the mail, run errands. Dinner and the evening on its way over. Too tired and not able to see so well for now, but working on building my resistance up. Joined the Y. Disappointed at the further delay on books from the job change, but expect to resume work directly on the Lucky Heart books. Decided on Strathmore laid paper for them. —Reading very little. Gerald sent *Gist of Origin;* read a bit.

10-22-75

Wind all the day. Eyes no better or worse. Now use a sulfa drug, and Dr. Meyer breaks it to me gently that I may have an allergy to something at work. My luck would have it be ink. So hope to know soon. Order paper tomorrow for Gerald's book from Aurie McGee, paper salesman for Irwin. Start on it next week. Talked with Randy and realize that I am not keeping the best of records on the press as I should.

Can see what I already know from the dates of the last few journal entries: I pick this up little of late. My working figures into this for more reasons than the physical. Learning to see myself as a printer and laborer. Getting a first hand taste of the public's sensibilities after a long absence. Had it before, then college. I continue to learn to live in the life long poetry. To say it again at twenty-five.

11-3-75

I have the first third of Gerald's book now printed. Slow going with the press, worn out after two years of overwork. A gray film of ink over the copy very difficult to control; trimmed the work is less distracted by such, figure it to be a final 10¾″ × 7¼″. Use a 24 pound Strathmore with laid  finish, 80 pound Nantucket cover. It begins to be passable, may be handsome when done. Have to print on the evenings and weekends; hard to make much headway, but I'm trying to finish the bulk of the work by the end of the coming weekend. It is possible. Hold up on title pages for LC catalog number. What I am aiming for is three of the books done by Christmas: most likely Burns, Brown, and Lally. The Trammell and mine soon after the holidays.

Troubled people here and, as heard, through the west. Two instances of cattle mutilations in Schulyer county. One young bull, and a black angus heavy with calf; organs removed. Crude imitations of the similar cases reported in the western states. The city busy about itself though. The numbers grow without work. More store and factory shutdowns, some friends move away. November so soon.

11-4-75

Ran through four more passes tonight, cut the first third to size and wrapped to wait collating. Fog this evening, weather moves in.

> how easy a knife the
> loosed the throat
>
> angus rolled to
> side on calfs
> weight   took
> the genitals
>
> finding them
> their own pasture

First chance or first snow, I clean the mantel in here of all but prescribed winter reading. Make it WCW, Olson, Zukofsky, get my *Making of Americans* back from McDonell, *Cantos,* and *Leaves.* Too ambitious, but possible and easier when set aside. Gerald's sensibility I suppose, think of seeing his NYC apartment and small shelf. The move from my hours now, and reading if to be will have to be small, consistent bits. Last hour.

11-5-75

Gerald's book a good half done tonight. Worked to 9, then supper with Ray, and then saw Greg Williams on Front Street. So. Getting through the book. Tomorrow already Thursday, and I wonder if I will finish by Sunday; perhaps. Aim for it.

little wing

11-6-75

Justis Perigo, look for more on him. First white settler in the area. Built a school first thing, building still standing in Fall Creek. This is a little more starting in me, long absence from journal, and history work. But anything. Finally getting where I can think and work at the shop. Settled into book printing which also gives ease of mind. Mean to mark a few of the things learned, try for more.

11-13-75

Finally winter, 20's tonight. Steve and Seibert dress seven ducks upstairs. Blue bills, large dinner to come of it.

Five more passes and ⅔ done on *Letters.* Have to spend some time on the house, caught at the end of Indian summer; house gives away the heat. So, windows, doors, and some yard work. In bed early tonight; shop work especially tiring last two days.

I see Michalea. Longer than either would have guessed, but getting in ways comfortable. Little time for her, seeing someone a space in all other works. A work.

Iliniouek   Illinois man

Cadillac, cadillac-cheep,
cheep cheep.   Not paper,
at the shop it is
best, or job. For
the customer better than
they know, but for
printing how

11-17-75

I look and see a few months, and I am almost four years in this journal. Judging from the pages, this one good for another four. Had hours this evening to work, but still resting from the weekend. All day Saturday for a trip to St. Louis and there hours fiddling with the binder we were to buy. Floor model a year old, a bit too erratic. Some called-in salesman who couldn't figure it out. Check its bed. Then, last night we roasted the seven blue-bills. Many friends, plenty of food; the day warm again. Chance to see everyone before the cold weather, ice.

Milk Poem

hard calving   herds
lactation not there   these
from the poor corn year
down stalks   gooseneck
stalks
would be the cutworm
circled   milk

*

not spilled ever on
floors wood   earth
by lips

any milk
needed

11-24-75

First real snow today. Nearly an inch now by the midnight. Just home from visiting with Ray at the youth home with Randy. Really busy with Valley, work at the shop, and trying to finish *Letters.* Got our binder today. Just need to finish the printing. Thursday and Friday off, so full days to print. Maybe bind first books by Sunday. Also waiting for the repaired cut I use for foil stamping from Columbia. So much to do, lean to the works.

11-30-75

Long holiday, work down. Late in bed before working again tomorrow. Gerald's book is very nearly done; the text is finished and ⅔ collated. Only title sheet, cover and trailing flysheet production note to print. Thursday in Chicago, hope to carry some completed. Will aim at this; still want to get a start on Bo and Michael's books before Christmas. —

Cold. Had eight inches of snow for Thanksgiving, gone now in the warming weather/rain, turned cold tonight.

Also got the repaired logo back from Columbia. Imprint back cover in gold. Have to figure the cover. I wanted to use a 17th century Venetian border, but may not. Still shopping. Tomorrow.

Sit up looking at typefaces.

1-3-76

Saturday afternoon, cold. Take a moment to sit with

journal. Last days of the holiday, and I try to gather myself and house. December was the most demanding month I have had in many. Worked mostly days and evenings and weekends. I did finish copies of *Letters*, took some to Chicago. Anania was impressed as were others. My own feeling being one of exhaustion. Tired of the grind, and so little done in a given period of work that it took what seemed forever. But did get a few done. Also finished a pressing job at the addressing shop just before the trip to Texas. Michalea came to stay and is still. The holiday trip was more tiring than usual. Still getting over. While away, I decided to apply for school in the fall. Thought about as many of the sides as I could, came up with the move. Michalea also applies; we will try to stay together. Only applying for two schools, so may not go. Getting an assistantship is essential which also cuts down on my chances. I've been out of school long enough to no longer know if I have a good resumé or not; guess the readers of resumés are the ones who decide. But try Hopkins and Brown U. Won't send any of the *Lee* poems, only *A Quincy History*.

Saw Burns and Trammell for the afternoon one day in Texas. Gerald looking good; unemployed, but getting healthy. Bob also in fine shape, trying to organize some massive fine arts show in Dallas. He could do it. Met at a gallery at SMU where there was an art show Bob pulled together: Dog Show. Some good pieces, strong show altogether. Also met Tim Coursey. Very fine craftsman: wood, metal, leather. Saw pieces of his work at David's; the Searcys in Mexico. Gerald pleased with the book, took him ten and brought back signed leaves for the lettered edition.

Mother with a collapsed vertebra, in pain but not to be kept down. My brothers both getting so tall. Gary to graduate this June. No college, not interested. Can't blame him. Dennis still wanting to be a cop, had to talk, but hard to tell if he is serious. Grandparents age very quickly now. Nanny, bless her, is getting crazy. Cutting her clothes up. Mother had to take her scissors away from her. —High prospects for the new year. The money problems that are cornering me will resolve themselves, though I can not see just how at the moment. Will get through. I would change my job if given the chance; the more I learn of the place, the less I want to be there. They have been good to me, however. What I need is a good dose of luck. Overdue. Overworked, know how it feels to be too fatigued to begin to write. But think, and won't let it go.

1-7-76

About 7 degrees all day. I'm still cold from trying to start the car this morning. Try to plug it in tonight.

Serenade

my ink hands on the
sounding board   such
a cold day

to play the board
sitting in to it
the music that is
heard through house
to play for music
and not effect to simple

and hand touch plays
a broom or anything
suddenly to the wires
and hear it   a printer
from shop

for Michalea

2-8-76

Seems the weather to break into 60's this week. Snowed three inches Thursday on my birthday. Quiet days, in work and evenings also. January such a good month for the work. Enough copies of Gerald's book finished to start sending out. No response, in general as yet, to those first few. Today finished another forty. Would the rest before the end of the month.

Twenty-six now, and four years journal. Not so many pages to show, but I feel good about the way journal has ordered my senses to verse. Scraps on paper during the day, but until taken here, just that. Thinking in line and ear. Almost abject.

2-9-76

Now February. The next months seem full enough. The fall close, prospects of school. If things don't work around that way, expect to pick up work with the press. If not school in the next couple of years, then a long trip in that time. Before 30. I have become more secure in my sense of poet here since returning from Baltimore. Feel confident, to use that word. Perhaps confidence only becoming less intimidated by the things I don't know. Time factor, in intellect, manageable. Not always.—

No magazines make sense. Curious to find myself held so toward them now; I want them to be good, but am disappointed. Aside from the books I'm working on, the new work isn't coming by me. Every now and then the random ms. out of the pile that would make a breath. Send a letter.

2-17-76

Quiet evening. Michalea out babysitting, and I am home from work today. Sore throat, first absence for health from the shop this winter. Spent the day sleeping and doing title pages for *Letters.* In last few days I have received the first word from the book mailings. Strong letters in favor of the work, most notably the Stafford. Also an interesting one from Vincent Ferrini who also wants me to publish a book. Would like to read the ms. but just can't take on any more work. Probably piss him off, but can't. Just got a $96 composition bill for Bo's book, $85 in my book account. If my luck holds, some money will happen along.

3-31-76

Saw a basketball game this evening with Steve Irwin. Finally finished a mailing for a new account at the business; looks like I can possibly get back to work here at home and on the books. Only the 250 covers to print, all of those to bind; collated nearly all the remaining signatures. I have not finished by the end of the month as I wanted, but I am in good stead as far as the work before and aft is concerned. The new month will see the conclusion of Gerald's and the beginning of the Brown book. Perhaps finish it altogether. Michael's will be in the hands of the typesetter; it's better to say composer now.

I learn of a friend who has a job as a barge hand on the Illinois River. Joliet to Alton. A possible answer in the event of no grad school. Not so romantic as it might seem. Work on-off six hours, work for 30 days, pay throughout according to Doug Smith. Made $18 a day on the first trip, $20 the next, up to $22. Then $26 and beyond to mate. Only captain then.

3-8-76

a womans washing face heard
through the kitchen a circle
accepts all the light

*

pipes house
singing

means to be so
for in kind
cupped   handed water

3-10-76

Much seeming to have happened but little to please
save the music. Saw Tony Williams and his new Lifetime
band twice over the weekend at the new club, Catacombs.
Actually it is the old Quincy Casket Co., a better name. Both
nights well received, the music excellent. Last night saw Luther Allison there, the best I've ever seen him. Almost all
blues, tremendous. It begins to appear that there is a place
here where quality music can be seen (and afforded).

Otherwise things dismal. While taking my apron off at
the shop my glasses fell and shattered. Can't see well
enough to work, cost also an unwelcome event. Suzy, the
woman who does my typesetting, broke her wrist, so another delay on the books. I had hoped to turn it to my favor; she
is going to give me a few fast typesetting lessons, and then I
will give it a try. I will save money, but now can't work until
new glasses are ready. Shoots the weekend. Newest revised
plans for work are to get the rest of *Letters'* cover printed,
Trammell's sampler printed, and get a start on Bo's book.
With me typesetting, I may push printing back a bit, to get
Michael and Trammell's books done. Can't figure the time it
will take. Already March and little to show for work on the
books. My strength at a low. Know the lights.

3-28-76

hours made similar
for time

*

old ink used
used or not
skins

to platen
tray on rollers

to begin all
the same to the air
thicken and skin

paper topping new cans

Nearly April, little to show for the books. Proofs for Brown's book returned and only one legit typo, three changes Bo wants. By the end of April, I should be able to put a copy in his hands. Have a cover drawing for the book, Gerald's goat. I should decide the paper, perhaps gray. And at least a more easily printed cover stock, and won't forget title on the spine.

In Carl Sauer

plants kept before
dishes   bowls made
pottery coiled
in answer to basket

we would keep
the animals

husk held first
seeds not hand

5-22-76

Sit with journal. Since last, a small performance. Pleasant enough except for the dancer; Michalea and I strike a partnership to buy a house. An offer made and accepted. Down payment to contend with. Work on the books inches. ⅔ of the Lally book composed by Eddie Hames. Trammell sampler cover thrown out and start over. Brown book still needing cover and title sheet, paper in though. 30 more *Letters* bound today—all covers printed. Wish I had a week for the press. First week of June drawing near. Most likely get the Payson history book at work this week also. Plenty to do. As always, my sense of work. To say chores, not badly. How else done.

6-9-76

Finally hot. Today June, the middle of the year. Late garden just in today. What was still possible, okra/squash/tomatoes. The things I eat each year. Last one at this house, close the new house deal at the end of the week. The things that have happened in the past weeks, now a moment: first few copies of Brown's book finished and taken to Chicago for a book fair; Gerald's *Letters* a surprise favorite at the fair, and he sends a page to the new book. Labor heavy at the shop as the time is on for printing the Payson history book. Helping a group of people; Gary Butler drawing houses, large book, to be bound in Jacksonville.

Pulling the small mulberry saplings from the garden. This is not a nursery, but a garden. Shirley comes to the garden. Okra row down one side shows the side off, moves toward the house the deeper into the yard. Hoe the fish heads here. Those left after the cats. In the new house, our share to visit.

6-10-76

To live in a town to make the books. Not as simple as giving the books away, but to place in hands. Leaves made for palm. The women at work will read if given, addressed.

6-20-76

I finally finished the Payson book Friday after a four-teen hour day. Hardest week I've ever worked as a printer, but finished title seems legible, clean, and ink is mostly consistent throughout. The weekend spent at auctions buying for the new house. Nice oak pieces at reasonable prices, some dishes, chairs, even an old copper boiler, Atlantic, to hold kindling.

Word from home generally good. Gary moving out with a job in Mesquite. He said I had made it, so he could too. Mother and Poppa working as hard as ever. Only Nanny having to be tied to her bed now, falling too often and finally "having lost hold of her mind." Grandaddy in bed all the time, played out. But he is still talking about getting back to Dallas, painting the house he will never see again. It is better that he has plans I think; hope that I do.

6-23-76

Much of the house packed and moved. Just getting into the office tonight, most difficult as I don't want to lose track of letters bills, etc. Healthy tho, the move.

> as yard became turned
> in garden by side
> of house each years
> spading to surface
> childrens men and
> toys todays cobalt
> marble given for
> Michalea

carp pieces
well dirted
to tell tails
fan from the
head or clod
only lighter
by fork

---

varietal
that these are
of purpose orchard
more apples
for canning
better in storage
from conscience
less ones eaten
from the tree
but all to be so

7-6-76

In the new house. Bone tired both. But sleeping and eating here. Rooms soon to shape. And rest.

7-10-76

Just past two weeks. The downstairs pretty much settled, my office nearly. In the office now, already hot here this morning. It is the small room at the back of the upstairs, over the kitchen. Hung shelves on the outside brick walls. Most everything in here, just needs to order. With time from the shop, I have been moving last things and working outside. Yard neglected for several years; I uncover the brick sidewalks. Uncover the brick apron that extends around the house, and unearth a walk from the house back to the barn which was completely covered. Hot work, but it, more than any other labor, yields more immediate pleasures as progress piles up, or stretches out in front. Have had an urge to work in journal but have not. Want time for reading and bookwork, but have not. This will change, but a house in disorder takes all. I have the feeling that there must be changes in most of my labors, job, business, and press work. Long for respite from the daily routine of the last many months. A prospect for work elsewhere is promising, but we are poor and Michalea without means. This must underlie the anxieties: hers and unhappy, no one hiring. This and other pressures nearly enough to take the pleasure out of labor. Realizing in creation, all conscious and larger concerns at work, but that disorder the unconscious method of some, the movement toward order mine. Order not artificial, though precision another sense. GB would be. The light exists in the world. That there window's glass and waters through it.

                    old glass best
                    for pictures and windows
                    alike   the sheets
                    ever differing

                    movement to each

                    save the one
                    replaced broken
                    one of four in
                    white sash and frame
                    flat to clear cleaner

                    how each lights

8-1-76

Cool Saturday night
after a rain Friday. Long week back at work after the work
at home. During the week Bob Brown, Bo's father, died of a
heart attack. Some phoning to locate Gerald for them. Sad
to say. As it happens their wanting him to fly up for the
funeral, but his not being fit. They did well as Bo said today
on the phone. His father hating the doctors, beat them, dead
in the ambulance. Not embalming, and they build the coffin
at home.

Our house coming along. Nearly finished upstairs,
painting and erecting a false wall in the hall still. Our patience with this still holding. What is done will help in the
renting, we are very poor now. No work for Michalea and
small reserves gone. Through this I try to pursue the books.
Nearly a hundred of *Letters* bound in the last two Sundays
and 50 of Bo's. Expect this to be a good month for the press
if I can do something each day. It is possible, I believe, as
the work is spread all over town: binding at the Valley office, trimming and stamping at work, Trammell's sampler to
stitch at Bert's, more of Bo's at home.

Wanting journal. If it is so, as Gerald would say, that I
write in sameness, then what I need is more. Wanting to do
the poems that are now as all the others. Their writing.

8-12-76

To come up
the back way

through the kitchen
the stair we
open   had nailed

the new house

I come to
the journal coy
straighten

which new every
not enters as
then light

as live with one

The printer in meanings, pressman. Operator to pressman in the space, his printing the tickets well. So many of
the jobs to days as lunch, get the printing. And would but
for love of papers. The extra two dollars improve the index
to a cover. All the tickets valuable, otherwise. How this a
term in making books, cleaning the press well end of day.
Since mine, I have taught two others to run a press, and
what I have, would me.

Mark paper. So late in which the fibers would be
moved. Signed road is guide for those would travel, let the
mark be meaning first hands, feet, ships, horns. The most
easily fashioned and earliest are geometrical, but after the
curve in animals became oval, their eggs, and natural stones
cube. This marks paper. An image, by all around it or by
absence, in paper more water.

8-26-76

Hot and getting late. A disappointing day in that the
first real lead on renting the apartment upstairs fell through.
We got stranded in Payson with car trouble, then it started.
Home a bit late to meet the people, they returned and

backed out. First two days for the ad though, must give it time. . . . Trammell's sampler finished, all of them. Now have to do another run of Bo's as the last dozen I have turned out to be defective: collation mistake and I don't know how many got out. Very disturbing to me, but it had to happen to me given the manner in which I work. At present, the printing and stamping are done in one place, color work and embossing at another, stitching and trimming at another and binding elsewhere. Wasteful. Embarrassed that it happened and would repair. Piece written while driving to Chicago a month or so ago on a scrap of paper.

> after each sleep
> an animal
> will set the
> body to form
> in stretching

> the turnip half
> eaten on the walk
> early near home
>
> a white center
> as its skin to
> purple shoulder
>
> what love would
> love an enteredness
> moved from one
> for one

That the work becomes smaller, or my seeing. It is not

enough to point to the longness of work hours and the difficulties of home, though the feeling is that only pieces are
managed, before it is broken off, thought elsewhere. Troubled. The verse is not happily new, or strong in the making.
I am for change in the life, soon. Better to bed.

Hard to be pleased. "Pangaean" last one that would
move me, that I have not been living to my work as needed.
Book work and press, these are not to satisfy except for
labors. I can work for the many, but to place above this the
poetry that I would. In the low, the times that are least di-
rected and in moments of stricken purpose. The feeling that
little or nothing has been offered, that I have less, none,
what I would. It is not a newness except that it does not
come in the reading of another's greatness. It is not
Whitman's that humbles me now, the day.

9-2-76

Take up the bricks
pick up the walks
the bricks beneath
the grass and between set
forms while the city
gives concrete
last brick street covered
where the mud ruts
where evened by clay

they put them down
again in old town to
build the neighborhood

the turnip I saw half
eaten on the early morning
walk better on brick
would concrete

9-26-76

Rained two days now, first such in so long. Last bit of the weekend, they go so quickly. Last week went to Freeport and Rockford to lecture and visit John Monroe. Most of two days spent driving, very good to be out in the country as I took two-lane blacktops most of the 500 miles. Some new work.

    the drawings I see
    in the cars of the passing
    train

        next

    as the named   fields
    in passage
                BoJac
    FS
    DeKalb
      wing ear American
    Pioneer
    Pride

        my mother said once
        of the few corn
        in beans and maize
        This is pioneer corn

    _____

        as flowers put
        next to the corn

beans next year   as
houses would keep
near the trees
they step down

---

palm oil
soy oil

petunias in Dixon
sustained

---

corn ears tied
to the mail
box post

ear tied to
the wagon for
the harvest
driven

(10-8-79 Stockton Illinois)
Lucy Miele Farm House/Finished poem.

These and I am feeling better toward work. I even got 100 copies of Bo's book bound today—cooled off enough to want heat. A man says $300 to get the fireplace in shape to use. Sold the Plymouth to Randy and got my 63 Olds. Going to bed to read; trying to learn to read once again.

10-11-76

Waiting for Randy before driving to Chicago. Mostly to see Dan & Elaine's new son, Isaac. Illinois Arts Council meeting tomorrow at 4 in Evanston with readings afterward at Amazing Grace. I will try to read nearly first, so I can leave for the drive home.

Bought two tons of coal, got the furnace going and fall becomes more evident. Life with one moving slowly, alive.

10-13-76

And returned. Isaac the son very beautiful. Took gifts for him. Know I am tired, found the poem I lost in the wash.

> what the car running
> in fine white
> rock of the drive
>
> limestone cities
> built on   town—hamlets
> the same in washes
> and bluff limestone
> sold it to the world
> on the river
>   smallest
> crushed rock white
> in fresh oil as
> if sunflower seeds
> not tasted

11-2-76

Soon we marry. 27th. Decided a week or so ago. Have made invitations, few plans, and now wait the weeks. Michalea has a new dress, and I buy a three piece suit I try to get cut to size, gray. Her brother throwing a reception, but too small for all friends so we throw the house open the 13th for a party with Bill & Carrie. Telling our friends to come to that if they want to celebrate with us. Never really made plans for my wedding.

11-3-76

Carter won. Bought eight tons of coal today, should carry us through the winter. Bill and I covered the windows with plastic all the day Sunday. Near as I can tell we are ready for winter. I have had to let everything ride the last two weeks while these tasks were attended. Still want to get Michael's book ready to print, finish mailing Bo's book. Much to do and still want to do things before the wedding. Family to be here, Poppa unsure. To be in Peoria next week also. Everything closing fast. Need a bath. Slowly reading, last month the Olson-Pound pieces, St. Elizabeth. I can only say for now that it is interesting Olson, seeing himself in EP. Had not been so aware of the trial. Michael and I driving past that hospital many times, never thought about it. Some funny things. —Pound's sense of self, surviving everything, drove Olson away according to the last few pieces.

12-20-76

Possibly the longest absence in the journal this time. I have read nothing, printed nothing, written nothing, at best managed to survive myself. We had a nice wedding with my brothers and mother, Lucile & Ben & Brian & Jack all driving up, many people from Chicago also here for the wedding. At the party we had the previous week, or was it two weeks, many friends appeared. Dan, Elaine, and child stayed with us; John McGahen and Barb Roth also stayed with us. After the Peoria readings and party, things swept us into the wedding. Left the next day for a week's honeymoon in Texas. Happy for Michalea to meet Poppa. Very enjoyable week visiting with family and friends (one night in Dallas, dinner at Gerald's small garage room behind Tim Coursey's with David and Jean Searcy, Bob Trammell and his friend Pat) until the evening before leaving. Car broke down in downtown Dallas; next four days were spent shuttling from one relative to another while being taken by unethical mechanics. Finally had to abandon the car to their care, drove home in mother's car. Left on a Wednesday evening at 7:30 pm. Quincy the next day at 11:45 am.

The trip and final car problems were very wearing after the wedding and all. I don't quite feel right yet, cold threatening, but I am holding on for the holidays and perhaps some rest. Michalea working evenings now as a cleaning lady, while I continue to manage the shop, work at Valley, and pursue a partnership in the new Gem City shop. Spending evenings as I can at the new place mostly putting type back into cases and cleaning up. Difficult not to get one's hopes up, but it looks as if a partnership is being formed between Randy, Geo. Hamilton, and myself.

Nearly forgot, I will begin teaching creative writing in February at John Wood Community College, two classes each week—Wednesday here and Thursday in Pittsfield. Each for three hours credit, each for $540. If I can land some visiting PITS weeks something that becomes more necessary each day. Too many things have become increasingly difficult as I work there, to no good purpose. For the new year I would settle some of the disorder of my life, so that I might pursue my verse better and enjoy Michalea more who I love.

12-27-76

It changes. All the printing, as the reading.

1-10-77

Cover and first few pages run for Eddie's *Flute Song*. He has put together a not so bad first one. "Punch in a Nutshell" by Gerald really fine, and Michalea's poems. He is building on things *Salt Lick* took the hard way, which is fair, already looking to the next. At the same time getting proof  copy of Lally knocked out to Gerald. Perhaps the ms. ready for print before too much longer.

Reading EP's *ABC of Reading* which is as the light, clear. Surprises me that I can read so readily; given the two or three pages I manage before bed or upon wakening. Isaiah Thomas' *History of Printing in America* just arrived. 1970 reprint of the 1810 edition with some additions. Thinking of using *ABC* to some extent in the courses, perhaps secondary text, at least handouts. Is especially good for what it teaches of Gerald.

1-12-77

Watching Eddie and the magazine in his hands. All printed, folded, and together in another day. He has chosen to hand work some of the illustrations, adding stickers, a card being cornered on the back page: it seems to be turning out as built on the types of technique in *Salt Lick*. I hadn't asked for this, but he looks at it rather as the way he prefers to do the work. Sometimes not thinking. When I would look at it and want to see it new; his silk screen very fine. Perhaps fooled myself. But he is thinking; it is his magazine, not mine. Just curious at close hand.

    any of us in close
    hand   out living
    the ones lived by
    continue
    to see it in another
    hand the moves
    of each hand

1-19-77

Two more inches of snow, work shut down due to furnace. A day at home, made lentil soup. Nice to sit for a time by the window.

> a gifted hand
> in turning
> the world
> the rain that would
> fall not for making
> anys corn spoil more
> than grown
>
> in agency of the wind

1-23-77

Just in Oklahoma before going into Missouri on the way back home. Had to pick up the car in Texas. Dennis ill and in the hospital. Very hard to write in the car. Bill driving as we head into an apparent snow storm. Light rain from Whitney to 4:00 this morning. Large falcon seen as well as a coyote.

A traveler's overtaking a traveler and one pulls to the shoulder. The roads built to it, and not in the absence of custom.

> one language and eaches
> the fruit in all tongues
>
> children lifted and held
> how said to   be heard
> pretty   the young
> given in hand
> bones or woodens
> for holding
> and to mouth

2-1-77

Popular Attention

In print, in the word, clothes one to wear. From the first such
sheets, papers to carry from the few to the several. The beauty
of intention. The Chinese and Persian posts, given way to the
Acta Diurna whose officialness seemed intended to gather public support for the actions of the generals, but when practiced in
quantity soon bowed to the better purpose. The quartos beginning to resemble those who made in content, past their licens-
ing. What foods surpass the public virtue of a country when
withheld, what laws survive. The paper of this town as a false
reply to needs, old money and an unthreatened domain holding
it up. How now any who would foster the new must needs
independent means of supply. The tradition of those who
would publish for less than talent, learning, and virtue older
than Thomas and more the tradition in America. Daye our first
and his unconscious *Psalme* a monument.

> For want
> the *New Light*
> in the day
> and the sovereign
> peoples
>   who would have
> others of own
> to speak and take
> these the word
> as love   and
> the cautious
> man for no less
> than trust would
> have it said well

Any less so in these time, belief wanting in a distance with our
sheets at once hollow. That we kill so well should ease, begun,
but for others who see. The voices of girls outside this night are
the bells of heart. And there is singing.

3-16-77

Out of the job finally, only days but it seems like months. New company near newer equipment, going to St. Louis this week to look at a press, and the idea of self-employment with a chance in machinery seems possible. New spring, garden soon. The turning of things in a life, such affecting. First changes in my spirit, to return to some clearer sense of home life; seems a call to more journal; and I hadn't realized that my not showing work to anyone had been going on for so long until Michalea said. Several months.

3-28-77

Rain for days.

First moves made with Cinda Awerkamp to legalize the press, a foundation. In hopes that books and pamphlets can be easier in the years, less susceptible to the whim of circumstances.

Some time spent out of doors Saturday. Blistered hand from raking, everything greener by the new day. Her tulips seemingly grown at night. Drove scrap paper crate lumber into the ground behind the garage with Bill & Carrie for a compost bed. In the air for hours.

> whose velvet leaf this
> grown close with the beans
> *fields own*
> little in town where
> the grasses choke it out
> fox tail better by the
> roads not quite city
> lambs quarter
> for pig weed
> whose better garden

4-17-77

To hear that word through
light,   voiced on ray,   just
our heat bodied.   Not secret
between us, an nearness.

A woman would sit with
the animals, and the man.

Days in the yard and shop. Suddenly summer and no
spring. So hot, what will August have. Our garden mostly in,
some things to wait past the threat of frost. Brussels sprouts
to taste better after a light one though. Apparently a time of
clear achievement for me, things getting done, in course.
Garden in better shape than when done alone. Bill & Carrie
also putting in things I hadn't such as chard and bok-choy.
Spent an hour or so in the north bottom cutting saplings for
bean poles with Bill. Much time of late spent north by the
river first getting stones for a terraced flower garden built
last week, now saplings. Usher in the new days that way.
Mushrooms shortly. Too dry, some up already. May get
some asparagus growing wild at Manny's camp on the bay.

peonie buds half-black closely
with ants every bush he has
seen said George and then

Carrie at the trail across
the walk   ants   their eating
the small pearls   surely sweet

May 15–77

Nearly a month, and a week in Mattoon, Illinois visiting classes and readings. Garden up and doing well. And arson at the shop. Someone broke into the back of the building and set a blaze under the stairwell. We were lucky not to lose the building entirely: thanks to the firemen and the anonymous boy who told them there was smoke coming out of the building. Ours was the third fire in a four block area in a two hour span, no connections other than those. We suffered structural damage due to fire, heat, water, and smoke; we also suffered content damage for the same reasons. Our presses and cutter are all rusted, the cutter perhaps out for good. The heat was enough to ruin the presses, rollers and perhaps warp some of the castings. Our insurance was sufficient for the building, but we were under-insured on contents. Bad break for us; all we have done the last two weeks is clean what we can, leaving much of it for the claim adjuster to see. It has thrown our timetable into the air once more. Our new offset equipment ordered, now we must delay its arrival in order to prepare its space properly. Trying to be aggressive about turning this in our favor, but our success remains to be seen. Bad break.

The week in Mattoon was hard, but worthwhile. Saw four/five classes each day excepting the last. Curious to find myself talking about language in each class, deliberate finally. Also leaning on Pound while doing so, his *ABC*. But more over the individual language, set by so many factors that at best are variable in their circumstances. When said repeatedly, the feeling to me of correctness. Williams and his foot variable to breath, but that in ways almost too self-conscious a mechanism when what you eat, where you live, what you hear, who raised you, what's been taught: all these determining language. All determining breath which was his legislator. Ordinary Gerald's word, common mine. For each.

May 22, 1977

It seems more travel this month than for a long time. Away from Quincy another three days this week in Chicago. My best trip to that city of late. Stayed with Dan and Elaine and child. Sunny good weather for seeing a few friends; didn't catch a few like Dick owing to being in and out at odd times, but Angie and Judy Varias came over the night before I left. Angie gave me a copy of the new album he is on; very fine swing jazz, a real start for him. The surprise of the trip being a chance to see the Tutankhamen exhibit at the Field museum. I knew it was to be there and thought about trying to manage seeing it, but had little hope since the lines have been so long and I had little time during the day. A friend of Dan's had tickets for an evening lecture and closed showing. Incredible. So curious to be moved by such strange and beautiful objects so far away (3,200 years). Awed at the fine detail achieved and at the sight of these things. The furniture nearly as interesting to me as the jewelry and larger golden pieces. From pictures, I saw a large bed or couch they say which was not part of the exhibit, Hathor. Would like very much to see one closely. They are made after animals, the legs front and rear as a large magical antelope or cow, its body covered with "club" card-like designs.

Home and trying once more to gather things in order. The shop still disoriented from the fire, and as yet lack of insurance claim. Very hard to pursue even simple tasks in the situation; we try for progress.

6-3-77

Very hot days and work at the shop. Carpenter started today; we still are pressed on all sides. —Sending a few poems out. "Pangaean" and two pieces of journal in a recent *Chicago Review*. Michalea saying my first publication since she has known me. Two years; surprised it has been that long. Curious to see those pieces in print as well. Cards from

Burns and Bo both saying they think the work good. A review of *Two Kids* in that same issue by Julie Siegel.

6-12-77

Quiet night and end of a hectic weekend. For the new week, we should learn if we have bank backing for the business, place the completed order (send money) for equipment with Detroit, and finish the new pressroom/darkroom. Tall order, but one to be met.

Also working on a room for Michalea, usually a few hours in the evening. It is the old summer kitchen behind the house. Going very slowly, the wood being refinished; such a small room with two windows and three doors. Nice to do the kind of work it is; almost all labor for now and just as well with little money on hand. Hoping for order soon; hope to put some form to the looseness of purpose of late. Not for a lacking of things to do, but better to move on each without neglecting all else. June nearly half away, settling into it now.

6-29-77

I have painted and patched walls at the shop for two weeks each day. Even last weekend painted a room at home, just keep doing it. Just that the feeling is of worthwhile labor rather than standing around mired in pointless conjecture about one thing or another. Another way of looking is to see it as saving the shop money which can be spent on other things better done by others: shelving in several rooms, added support under the floors. The work is hard and in such heat, but it shortens the day. Little strength when home and then usually spent by Michalea. Very soon Tom and Gladine from Texas for a visit, his first to the house, and we try to do some work in preparation.

The garden very wealthy. We've canned eight quarts of green beans and a little zucchini while also eating the same several times. Still eating chard also, and tomatoes this week, I believe. We ate squash flowers and they are good. Much like wild mushrooms in the way they are dipped in egg and crumbs before frying. Pumpkin flowers are said to be better; we will plant some before long.

Again the summer and little of poems in this journal.

7-7-77

By candle with the power out. Storm at the end of the day with hail, quietly cool. Only day this century in sevens. Michalea on the bus to Chicago to see Tut, stay with Dan and Elaine. My parents came and left. A very pleasant visit, nearly too short, but Poppa anxious as ever to leave. Hard for him to sit, even in Whitney while there.

7-15-77

The new press is installed, proof press also. Through the hottest week, 100° days; we hauled the presses through a narrow walk across the back yard and up the steps. Not much left to the steps, still a camera and platemaker to come through the same area tomorrow. Randy and I will drive to Millstadt to pick up a pair of galley cabinets and a saw. The shop suddenly begins to take form.

New Hamada is complicated in ways the other machines I have used are not. The hope is that in a few months I will be proficient. The difficulties of being the only one in town (Hamada), no local pressman to look to, is a challenge. Just today we were given the first job of size for it: Payson Old Settlers pamphlet. Also a call from Chicago: Illinois Arts Council willing to give me $500 to do the Lally book. As to being on the press with it by the end of the month, now unsure of my abilities. But it will be this year that I finish Lally and Trammell for the break. And mine in the winter. A chance, if taken, to clean up loose ends before foundation work begins in earnest. Actually the IAC grant may be the first monies for the foundation, but still the question of financial records and closing out the old account. A fresh start at hand sooner than I thought.

> my
> squash flower eater
> please
>   miss baby bell
> I'll ask you just
> one more

8-4-77

Rest. Where there was confusion and frustration at the shop these last weeks, there begins to be order now. All of the vital pieces of equipment are there, a shakedown due for each still, but we have what we need immediately. Fitting shelves and storage what is left of space.

Michalea and I ease away to Chicago tomorrow night for a few days. Staying with Angie and Judy. Dan, Elaine, and boy arrive here Sunday night for a month. Dan returned to Chicago immediately for one more week of work, but return as we leave.

8-10-77

First sign of the weakness of heart. The constant of last months to tire me, body and heart at times vacant. I try to listen to music for spirit, sit to write. Blue suddenly at times. Anyone.

8-24-77

Work the constant, but it begins to be done. I have spent hours where needed through the night at times, but running the press, making it work. This and work at the house has made for the most active period, day to next, in some time. The pressure begins to adjust to the achievements, and I am, I feel, nearly to the top of a climb. So much ahead for sure, but I have done so many things just now that were burdensome beforehand that the feeling is one of achievement. Good. Perhaps I can again think past the immediate and enjoy.

Dan has the new book/record shelves up barely, finish work still. Gerald writing little of late and again ill, worried. Bo writes and works on "The American Wing." Michael does not understand the constant (true) delays with his book. Trammell moved again and is not to be found. Feeling my studies as printer have moved me further away from my writing and friends in same. Hoping that changes with the fall and winter. Truly.

10-12-77

Rain into evening. Michalea out for the moment, quiet time for me. To Chicago Thursday for a meeting and reading with others in the group the Council books. Visiting schools here three days in November but no other readings this year. This is fine with all the labor ahead. Little to say with all for now, still books. Letter from Bruce Andrews recently who saw my work in *Chicago Review* and liked it, grammar against texture. Sent him some poems, but see few poems in these pages for the last six months. It would seem a time when much is taken in though little would out to a paper.

10-18-77

Uneasy day, brief illness. Some from drink the previous night, more likely reaction to the hardness of the Chicago run. Enjoyable trip though in several ways; met Jean Thompson and John Jacob who both will be spending two weeks in residence here later in the year, good. I was approached to do two readings in Chicago later in the fall, one with Lally at the Body Politic. Stayed with the Variases. —

For the briefness, the reading good. Left journal at home, so did some newer things from notes, read some *George Washington Trammell* which was very well received and filled my spot in what is a round circle of writers in the group. Always a few I like especially, though Lucien Stryk very bad in reading things from his new book. Recently back from Japan where he went to complete the book, he read a poem in particular about 500 victims of a mid-air airplane collision. Very lame, and he falls into the trap of thinking the significance of the death makes his writing about it valuable. Plus the misfortune of his repeating ". . . five hundred dead . . ." etc. Sad; I had liked earlier work.

I see this and look toward my work where getting it clear about a small thing in life helps to place significance in its position. A poor argument would be that since we all write of experience, to write of events that affect masses or larger parts is "politically" correct, or the individual in solitary movement lends direction. My writing of light and saucers and heart egotistical? Perhaps, but important how each. Imagine writing of Quincy and wanting to speak to people.

> some and part the notions
> your not speech to my hearing
> the movements in touch from
> learning against
>
> as cooking for each and not
> each food
>
> a threaded fiber
> through sweet potato
> yam and plantain
> these and other
> hold a heart meat
> what we eat and love

Art And Squirrel

we two left from
the lunch again
to work and the shop
the cat seeing between
the tree

and walk a squirrel
his thought dinner
after eating both up
the tree the dying elm
last leaves

not thick enough
not to see their
circle   the trunk
the cat suddenly
clumsy and foolish
to the chiding

clicking of the squirrel
cats only knowing
one way down   even
if he had

Incorrect.

9-20-77

Looking through, there might be roughly as many as
fifty pieces in the first book of *A Quincy History.* Quick

count, journal and poetry. Probably work it down to just below forty, but still a few of the ones yet written in the next month or so. It would be good to make first moves though before too long. —Final proof of *Catch My Breath* mailed yesterday, should be returned soon. Begin October ? No way of telling, but clear to see soon. —Printed a pamphlet for Gerald, *The Updater's Manual.* Technique and theory for correcting composition with the computer where he works. Gerald sentences. A job at the shop; hope that his company comes across with money, otherwise taking advantage of him. On the phone, Burns saying this his third and I've printed.

9-24-77

Chapman

"Who in a long packe
which he carries for the most
part open and hanging
from his neck before him
hath almanacks and books
of news" or less for sale

would not live well to the world
by labors   mind
the accounts of saucers and cats
    kept   a   hand
in learning

First from an English Dictionarie of 1611 and perhaps one of many if I follow an amiable idea to do a small number of such accounts. Maybe distant cousin of a Description of Trades book as well. A second volume of *A Quincy History.*

10-1-77

applewood
too wet
still moving
top ones for the
rest below

then to see
the slug
some salt
dull green and beautiful
in beaded skin

once one
then the rest
slightly beside
underside of a log
a town

and cricket
a city

10-20-77

Nearly the month. Michalea bathes, and my next early this cool morning. Our furnace in need of $400 worth of repair, heavy blow. We've made it so far without heat, but unlikely much further.

Work at the shop moves on. Sometimes difficult to see our progress; still no wages. But the quality of the work improves slightly and first customers start coming back.

Lally ms. back with final corrections; hope to work on it this weekend. Once warm in the house, hope to resume many works.

11-6-77

By the end of the day, the house ready for winter. Windows covered, furnace working.

Difficulties. Work slowed at the shop. This makes for a desperation of sorts while the figures look promising. Eddie has lost access to the composer in the midst of finishing Lally. Do not as yet know how to get around this one. There is also an end of the month deadline on expending the grant monies I received for materials for the book. So this the next in a too long list of problems, postponements, and downtime. I take direct responsibility for most of these delays; even the latest would have been avoided if we had gotten on with it. I will never do another book the way I have done this one. There is learning from the way this one has proceeded, but again, never like this. The Trammell planned for soon after will most likely have a considered timetable designed to eliminate foreseeable conflicts and use more readily available equipment.

I also feel badly about my lack of work on the ms. at this point and know no other acceptable way out except to finish.

11-21-77

Just home from helping unload furniture in Warsaw for Dan and Elaine. They are just getting into the house before snow.

A long week and now the weekend over too quickly. Tuesday evening we leave quickly for Texas, and in many ways this as other trips: pick up and leave things just to get away. The middle of the week I visited classes at junior high, senior high, catholic high, and college. Some fifteen hours including a reading at the end. An encompassing reading: read much of the *Robert E. Lee* ms. which I had not read for years in some cases, parts of the *Circle* and *House* sets. Also the sampler and journal and new pieces. Apparently well received. Schweda afterward said of the later things that he saw me in a technical phase and was anxious for me to get through it. Hard to say how he means, but in a few senses understandable. I think later things harder to hear and hold for most. My feelings that the work has been weak the past year, only two poems to please. Hope for the best, try for a way to work through all there is. Apparently I have not as yet learned how to manage my personal needs with home and business. Calls for a fresh look at each. And nearly the end of a year.——

Try to see Gerald and Trammell and David next week if only briefly.

11-30-77

What I had not seen
trying to let the cat in
the evening before
was the birds head
she was playing with

watch a cat push
something found on floor
with its paw
if not eating they
like this

Home from Texas and snow storming. Still weary from travel. Fine holiday. Spent one day with Burns & Trammell. The grandparents over for Thanksgiving and Willie Maude also. Long drive back.

Arson probe

Draperies soaked
with fuel oil

Firemen found definite evidence of arson in the fire which gutted the first and second floors of the Credit Control Services offices, 520 S. Fourth, late Tuesday night.

First Assistant Chief Jack Schneider said the state fire marshal's office had been notified and that state officials were expected to investigate.

The Fire Department officers said it based its suspicions on draperies found in the building, obviously soaked with fuel oil but not having burned. These were curtain materials, the department said, which had been taken down, soaked with a flammable material and then laid end to end up the stairwell from the second floor to the attic.

The draperies were behind a closed door, however, and firemen prevented the flames from reaching that point in the building.

Appearing to start on the first and possibly the second floors, the fire had spread over a wide area when firemen arrived. The flames virtually gutted most portions of both floors.

The building is owned by Dean S. Slough and was used as offices for Credit Control Service.

Slough said the fire "is highly suspicious, but I have no idea whatever who might have done such a thing."

He said it's still too early to determine what material can be salvaged. "My business records, however, are safe," Slough said. "They're locked into computer tape."

Slough said his loss was covered by the insurance but declined to give a figure on the amount of coverage.

Quincy Herald Whig, 12/7/77.

12-13-77

Some of the worst time of recent memory for me. One week ago a fire swept the old shop and with it Lally's ms. on tapes. The tapes survived, but I, as yet, do not know the circumstances of their contents; they were exposed to extreme heat and cold. They were found in a box on Suzy's desk frozen in water from the firemen. I have been a little in shock about this, I guess. The press at work is disabled, and still I have to get work out. Each day weighing heavier on me it seems with little to ease the strain. I have not told Michael yet, waiting to know the outcome of the tapes. Working very long days at the shop; have worked very long days and many nights since back from Texas and before. I can not help but feel that everything is heading for a climax of some sort, perhaps quiet, but a resolution to everything. It worsens.

12-15-77

More of the same. Suzy says next week we should know about the tapes. Doubtful their survival.

12-26-77

It has been a grim holiday, but it seems to lighten with the hours now. The tapes for Lally have survived in their blackened cartridges and mother's out of the hospital, her lungs nearly clear. Here at the desk and straighten it, the room. Try to let things assume their order once more. So concentrated have the days been that I have retreated to a place of cautious watching. Not wanting to do any thing while out of balance. So. Perhaps the break I have waited. Cleaning today.

12-23-77

Each Turning

eagerly into hand
though

we take them up
into the body and thinking
whats hurting and touches

1-4-78

New year. Everything over and it starts again. Work heavy duty with George in Vienna; we keep it going. Figure

Slough building fire investigation continues

By PAUL COLGAN

Local and state fire authorities along with insurance investigators, are pressing inquiries into the arson of the building and businesses at 520 S. Fourth Owned by S. Dean Slough.

Deputy State Fire Marshal Keith Ellis said chemical samples of the incendiary used have been taken for analysis.

The Quincy Police Department reported definite suspects in the case with an ongoing probe of "good leads."

No determination of loss has been made, according to Bill Lyle, of Lyle Insurance Co., which carries the insurance on the Slough property and businesses.

Meanwhile, the four Slough companies dispossessed by last Tuesday's fire found new quarters at 711 Maine. Jim Coleman, a Slough employee, said efforts are being made to salvage as much equipment as possible from the fire-ravaged building.

"We know it was torched," Police Chief Charles Gruber said. "We also know what substance was used and where it was poured."

Although Gruber said investigators have good evidence on the arson, he did not elaborate, saying the details are crucial to lie detector tests that will be given.

A special investigator from Springfield has been called in by the General Adjustment Bureau, State and Eighth Plaza, which is assessing damages. A spokesman for GAB said the investigation is routine in cases where insured losses are high.

Coleman could not give any estimate of the loss incurred by Slough, but said it could easily reach $100,000, depending on the value of the electronic office and printing equipment lost, as well as the damage to the building itself.

The Slough building housed four companies, Business Management Corp., Credit Control Service, Alpha-Omega Printers and the National Reading Enrichment Institute.

Coleman said employees are sifting through files to recover records. The fire fused many together in clumps, he said.

Coleman and other employees of Slough strongly deny any implication that anyone connected with Slough's enterprises was involved in the arson. They report that a previous arson attempt on the building was passed over by local authorities as insignificant.

The employees are considering establishing a reward for information leading to the arrest of the persons who touched off the blaze. "We want to find out who did this," Coleman said.

Slough was out of town Tuesday and could not be reached for comment.

Authorities plan to meet with Slough and his employees later this week when Slough returns from his out-of-town business trip.

Deputy Fire Marshal Ellis said he wants to interview a number of people about the fire.

Slough and another employee left the building around 9:30 p.m. about two hours before the fire broke out, sources said. According to Coleman, nothing was amiss at that time.

The arsonists were believed to have entered the building after Slough left .

The fire broke out about 11:30 p.m. and was "raging wildly" by the time firemen arrived.

Quincy Herald Whig, 12/13/77.

the shop to either stand or fold in the next six months. It could go either way as I see it. Hope to get on with these Lally & Trammell books before anything happens; mine if I have the means then. Waiting still on new machinery to have the finished copy for Michael. He has not written, and I imagine him upset with the new delay as he must be. Sad if this changes our relation, more than already.

Michalea ill, but better and gone to Chicago for work. I will read there with John Jacob the 16th.

Sold the Oldsmobile tonight to a man I never met who asked for it at the door. Then sat and cracked pecans for an hour. Brown called to return mine of last night when I had finished *The American Wing.* Think it very good and warned him about editors wanting to cut. Figured them to attack the directly physical building, Hatcher to Bo just the reverse. Told Bo to cut the personal (what isn't) and concentrate on the building, "How To Build . . ." He was also having some unacceptance from the family. Told him it was very good that he wrote it. Too long and wonderful. First reading of length I have done in months. Last night picked up F. O'Connor because Michalea was rereading it. Tonight reading *La Vita Nuova* which Gerald sent. He said it was on the page. Beautiful, sturdy book printed letterpress on hand-made paper; Thomas Mosher made it.

a plywood star on our wall
has star five points larger
than my small hands

as someone saw one we
ours   having found it

ours   I sit to look
and see it as love

*

when we are not talking
we are not looking
to see what the other
does but slightly

1-16-78
Chicago

A reading tonight here. The few days here have been good for their distance from the shop. As constant as it is, I actually am less aware of its totalness until away. To visit friends is pleasant, and I am anxious for the reading. As little as it matters, it pleases.

The dirt and snow which are roadside
in passing, less white to the flesh
or hide color. Their living not to
their light but their life in spines
and backs and shape. That it
was one or several lying closely
as legs and feet to head to legs.

1-22-78

As Passing

the bath tub buried half
upright   in their yard

facing to the house with
iris brown down to the
ground with winter

to stand with it in a
moment away from the kitchen
they put it there perhaps
not having seen another so

*

elsewhere our living as
we together from what we
have seen and wanted

what to call your shrine

A past week of crisis. Seems that the most critical moments in the shop have passed, and from now we are resolved to continue. The press has been repaired and will either support the shop or close it. We have realized ourselves to the work in the shop and go on. Another two months with correctly operating machinery and we will see. I was prepared to close, but we try again. Randy is to compose *George Washington Trammell* in spare moments while I still await the Lally. I mean to complete these works.

The reading in Chicago surprising. Jacob apparently due to many weeks of school lectures and workshops was down; in his words, as I approached the stage at the finish of the reading, "Burnt out." As far as response, the audience very receptive to my older things, rolling in laughter even at moments unclear. John McGahen said I had them. Several old friends there which was lifting. Apparently I was more hesitant while reading more recent works and more than one mentioned it afterward. Enjoyed it and was strengthened by having done it. Met Julie Siegel who had attended; fine poet. After the reading I went with others to a bar nearby to catch a set of Dick's band, Blues Twisters. Will see them this evening as well here, in a few hours too. Had the good fortune to see Jimmy Rodgers and Big Walter Horton together, then later that night Guitar Jr. with the Muddy Waters Band and the Fred Below Band. Below solid as ever and doing some jazz with two saxes in the band, Marcus Johnson and James Smith. The trip in focus for me. Good talking with Dan McDonell and McGahen. Now, everything to do.

2-13-78

The past two weeks have seen George want out, name and change a price, and consult lawyers. I'm not at the shop as yet; Randy to pick me up directly. But all we can do presently is keep the customers satisfied with work; not looking for work, and I am sure the talk of our problems is deterring some printing. But George has abused and cheated us in more ways than I imagined and the outcome is uncertain. He asked for much more than the building and his interests are worth; by the other token, his offer to buy our shares is an insult. We have the best lawyer in town, but we have yet to see if he can help us. A clause in our agreement may save us: any partner wanting out can be bought out at a fair market value. The rub is if the building can be defined as equipment. We think so, as does the lawyer who drew up the agreement; that same lawyer would be called as a witness since oral evidence would be allowed. Can not write any more of it.

The worst irony is not having done any printing for Salt Lick. I put all my energies to the success of the business. So, since I am unready to move on any book, I am doing simple reprinting of envelopes, flyers, cards, etc. Not so satisfying. Not shaken in my thinking to have *Catch My Breath* and *George Washington Trammell* done this year.

Sweet Teeth

wrappers in the cars
after her

2-18-78

Evenings

your wings red
and black   my brown

the Japanese school girl
who threw down her life
said she passed the
entrance to heaven

and took the name of
her clothing out of
so many she was
three days unknown

the next thing said
about money   that
we owe it how
much on this one

2-19-78

Double Helix All Loose

double knit all snagged
outside the city
their new towns

when its considered
what we lose the scale
what is left and it is
walking

3-18-78

It's nearly over. Within two weeks we sign the papers
and close the transfer of ownership of the building and business. We have won. It was necessary to make the direct
moves to close the shop in order to get George to a reason-

able price; as a result of these moves, we have diminished our accounts and inventory. But the shop is to be ours. The next few weeks are to be spent in cleaning, hauling out useless equipment, furniture, stock ruined by the fire that was never discarded, and trash. We want to get the front room cleaned up especially as it is the one the public sees; it was bypassed in the earlier cleaning. It nearly begins.

When it looked bleakest with perhaps a few days before we closed the door, I called Dallas to see what the chances/cost would be of getting Trammell's book composed by Gerald at national ShareGraphics. In three days I had Gerald set to do the composition, funding from Ridge to cover it, and a surprise call from George saying he was ready to negotiate. It was not fast in the way it happened with each thing that was required. We faced George and held our ground until he relented, arranged financing through Manny, cleaned up all the printing for customers in order to keep their good will.

I received the Trammell, shot and stripped it, then ran most all of it in two consecutive days. Only a single pass in the text to do and then cover. Waiting for CIP listing from D.C. on that run, and am having to rethink the cover and binding. Gerald sent for his copy of the Lally ms. from Michigan. My copy of the ms. gone in the fire apparently; only the final proofs w/ corrections surviving along with the tapes. I hope to have the composition by the first of April. After so long it begins to happen rapidly.

Another

There is no squash like a book.
There is no dress like the table.
There is no jelly for ideals.
There is no monotone like a neighbor.
There is no Emily like her.

4-9-78

The movement of the parts for the moment clumsy, though there is sway. The situation of the shop rides above and below everything else. The closing date was removed to the 14th which is Friday while a last detail is cleared involving getting Hamilton out of a lease we all signed. Once the dealing with George is over, we can settle in to the only struggle that ought to matter, success or failure based on our work. Today I did some of the last trim painting in the front room which has been cleared out and cleaned, patched and repaired, painted. Dan is to redo the entrance hall a bit perhaps, the counter in the front room, and paint the windows outside. All this and I have been calling on customers in the mornings, selling a few jobs.

Michael's book set, and he has a proof while I have the original. By Wednesday he should call to give me his list of errors. I have had a rough time living between Michael & Gerald. Now I must make final incisions quickly to get at the printing. Had hoped for *a* finished copy of the book by the 4th of May for Chicago, but it will be close. The Trammell ought to get finished before then. Order cover and text/cover for *Catch My Breath* this week. The bulk of Michael's a problem I hope I can handle in a short time.

As for energies: have worked days, nights, weekends, mostly steady now for, for a long time. Pressures constant and nearly dependable. I sometimes think of writing, but usually at an impossible time. Plow it back. Put them under.

4-15-78

Saturday morning. House above for a time. I've lost my stride for the past week due to a bad cold which once out of the throat went into my lungs. Just nearly over it. Trying to prepare for the finish of the Trammell and beginning of *Catch My Breath.*

It will be difficult it seems for my relationships with

both Gerald and Michael not to suffer due to this book printing. I do hope never to be so positioned again, between any two; realize this threesome, including me, is not in many stretches common but perhaps is. I just feel it to be ultimately destructive to me. Perhaps all printing, but that still needs some proving. —Michael complains of Gerald's "arrogance" while Gerald curses Michael's "timidity–unprofessionalism." Each relatively understood by me in their seeing, just that I see flaws in each. Gerald assuming an intractable position in order to deal with what he feels bulk and his not trusting Michael to have ruthless final sight in the pieces. In some ways, correct. Michael insisting on some changes due to his hindsight for correctness which is not uncommon in work written some years removed, then printed years afterward. The obvious problem is in seeing it, and Michael wanting to address himself to all things not concrete. I see that I should have been more direct in my dealings with both in order to avoid, if possible, some of the actions of each (self-defense) and in order to preserve more of my energies for the work. At best, my sight distorted due to external affairs of shop/home, but now just wanting to carry through. Seeing this journal perhaps of little use if a document for me in another time if I ultimately perform the same, my soft edge in dealing with friends, respected.

Having a pair of finished new titles by May 4th looms more difficult all the while. I need to find another $250 for paper for *Catch My Breath* is all. Everything else covered. Should make final decision for Trammell binding this weekend. Study other books. Cover to be dark brown as intended; favoring a printed label at present. On white gummed stock, red border.

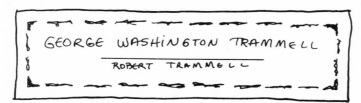

Printing on spine to be determined by method of binding. So slim a title to nearly rule out perfect binding. Otherwise a sewn signature.

Michael's also a problem in that there are fears of binding holding (his receiving a copy of Bo's that fell apart!) His book to be printed on a high bulk 70 pound text that will make for an 11 ounce/half inch thick title. Gerald suggests printing in cognate leaves, gather into four signatures, sew. Still thinking.

Castelaz's choice for cover is a strip to apply only on front cover, photos only. Title and author printed above.

White text, dark gray cover, salmon/pink printed title, spine. Photo strip black and white, on white perhaps light gray paper.

Gerald enjoying the collaboration on these titles and his typesetting excellent. Talks of mine now. It cheers me a bit as he knows and gives a little strength to think of what comes after all the work at hand. I can say or think little of it for now, as of the last year or more. Pleasing for a moment to think of a large typeface, 14/16pt. Blocks of text with spaces for devices (probably Goudy). Gerald asking if the marbled boards survived the move and winter. Have not looked, but believe so. Maybe this year, maybe into winter, or fall. Maybe I will have luck. Always luck.

4-19-78

I lay in the bed awake an hour this morning. Now evening. Michalea home from Springfield through the rain.

Probably the last of the corrections of *Catch* today to Gerald. Two hours on the phone late Saturday with Michael listing corrections, errors, inadvertences. Some of Gerald's errors, some Michael's changes (correct in either ms., galley, or both), some things he did not remember changing, some Gerald's changes. I admire the work Gerald has done on the book, knowing the difficulties now of setting from multiple sources, some of them untrusted. Just to get it out and over. Hope he decides to leave his name and credit in the front as we have eliminated the need for an errata sheet.—

We seem to go from one difficulty to another. A sudden setback at any time could put us under, knocking the few blocks we would stack over. Had to turn the heat on once more, 19th of April. It would seem that there would be a time when all points converge; or linear aspect of the daily adversities smooths. What we work toward. I do love Michalea.

5-18-78

In the month since last, the two books completed to the point of a dozen of each finished and away. With final corrections and changes cut in late Friday—April 30th, started shooting Lally Saturday. Worked steadily through the week; days, nights, early mornings to print. Left at 8pm Thursday May 4th with four copies of each protype. Dan helped me get those out, but miscollated the only misprinted sheet I did out of 50 passes (11–14); thought I had put them away. The books well received though, and they did look handsome. Few hours the night we arrived spent with Angie & Judy Varias; next night in Calumet City with John McGahen. Then home for May Babies. Never more apparent how much Randy covered for me that week. I misprinted (left some names off)—in the daze—an important job at the end that Randy reran. His first offset job. Too soon to talk about the books. Overwhelmed at work. Sewing Bob's books, maybe all; not liking wrinkled spine of *Catch My Breath*. Have to figure it out.

5-21-78

Listen to the clothes dryer. Thought of the photo of the dim laundrymat with them named: Cindy, Jean, and on.

Burns received the Lally and pleased; already talk of new titles to set. Hope before too long to start typing up *A Quincy History* ms. just to look at out of the journal. Also consider journal pieces for it. Did get two applications in for funds in the next twelve months—books and a magazine issue. Seems best to push in that way; *AQH,* a collection of poems by Michalea with artwork by Elaine Bohannon, and Gerald's ⅓ book of Spells. Then a separate magazine request. I will see what shape it would take and thinking of some contributors: Ahern for pieces of *Paradiso.* Also for a portfolio if Dan wants to do one. Would have the winter to work them.

No sewing or binding or collating this past week, but I shall finish some soon. Michael getting impatient I'm sure. Have to run some more covers for *Catch My Breath,* more cover illustrations also. Hoping to manage a large enough batch of each finished so I can get some out for review and distribution. David Wilk said send 50 of each. So many things pulling me, it will be hard to finish 100 of each before the end of June. Maybe.

> ways
> nothing out there not
> in here
>
> simple love a world so
> o many changing in
> the hour
>
> the logician safe
> from Africa white
> children's heads off

*

a river where two
banks   a people
where they are lived

Service

'sa   gladhand
for holding your air
or freely moving
among those together

my hands are your cup
of flowers and I put
the sweet potatoes in
the jars for you

6-5-78

The struggle with Hamilton is over. We signed all the papers June 1st and at the same time made the bank arrangements. Paid $15,000 for the building, property, business, and equipment. That day also the deadline for some large printing jobs, not allowing the effect of the signing to sink in. Randy, Betty, Michalea, and I celebrated the next night in high style, and the weekend was pleasant in ways that I had not known for a long time. It still is making its way in, the realization that it is over; better yet it is the start of the grind. I think it will work.

Friday to Chicago for a meeting. Should know by the end of that day how much we will have for the next year's work in IAC funding. Full funding would be about $3,000 for three books and a magazine issue. Trying to clear up my office (pit) and get some *Catch My Breath* done for Michael.

I have not heard from him since he got that first copy. Figure him to be busy, as I have been. An order from Phoenix Bookshop in NYC though; I imagine him behind it. No word from Trammell either; he is mad at the cover for his *George Washington Trammell*. Wanted large rugged letters and pissed at the label. Hope they like the books later. Gerald happy with both and ready to go again. He is setting Ahern's *Paradiso,* though at present Ahern is lost.

6-22-78

It has been difficult to sit with journal even a moment. 7 am and soon to work. But there are good things at work here as the summer gets off to a fine start. The list: both grant proposals were funded fully in Chicago to my surprise; the trip to the city also fun—saw Son Seals and met Bob Koester at his Jazz Record Mart; had lunch with him and also met the son of Sleepy John Estes. McGahen a very accommodating host.

Slowly it seems the atmosphere at the shop is changing for the better. Hopefully I will continue to ease enough to allow some enjoyment of the type missing from the beginning due to George. Not that there is not the stress of the work day to day, but there is less fear (at least for me) that we will fail from the external forces. Actually, the possibility of failure from external forces is still very real, but it will not be George and for that there is a feeling of triumph.

Have a self-imposed deadline of July 1 to have 100 each of the new books finished and it will be a last day affair I see. Mostly Trammell's to sew and trim; Lally needs the final printing of covers, some pages to rerun and perhaps ½ of the collating finished. Clearing the way for some sustained work on them now.

It is a new day.

7-3-78

Printed the rest of the Lally today. Quiet shop Sunday. Burned from the day before at Mary's farm with her parents and Randy & Betty, Elaine & Dan, Michalea. All day and much fun. Swam, made ice cream. It rained twice and that enjoyable except for E.J. My sympathies. Only a day each weekend to work & putting his tools away twice.

Have heard from Michael and Trammell. Hoping for progress on their books, all orders filled. Small reviews of both in a soon issue of a librarian's publication in Chicago. Both happy I think. Everything.

My parents visited and it was nice. Only very hot suddenly and very busy at work, both of us. They came in Sunday, then leaving Wednesday morning. They enjoyed it I believe.

This the first year in several that I have not planted a garden. We all put the manure in one morning, but since then not a part together. Tomatoes and okra from Texas last week. Summer majesty. I can hear the children on the corner in front talking and cussing. One boy making calls that are meant to be heard, but unknown. Girls too.

July 18, 1978
July 24, 1978

Say Them

the hats of the village
women mark them
married and those not
but ready

       elsewhere
the walk   beads
tobacco   ocher   dance

dress   hair your way
even now

otherwise ones not in hats
still the beauty

---

what is easier
if all hardly
whats possible

dinner with you so
hard I eat most all
things you eat few
the few you eat not
always

8-1-78

what is easier
if all hardly
whats possible

dinner with you so
hard I eat most all
things you eat few
the few you eat not
always

I ate potatoes for
breakfast when a boy

most always but not now
have changed and think
less of my eating but
think of you your
for breakfast there
is tea

Long entry due. Pace of weather and work has made journal work difficult past its normal contours. Did get a small package of books to Michael which eased him some; tomorrow night Eddie Hames and Mary Miller to help me get another batch further along. But all printing finally done on the two now. So only the hand work and bindery. Waiting on Randy for more Trammell labels which hold back many. In the midst of a heavy month of work at the shop, I will try for getting large numbers finished of both this time. Just do it.

The first board meeting for the foundation was held and came off without major snags. Janet Brown was a house guest with us that weekend. Very amiable woman. Long full life thus far, and she continues. Basically the meeting was a first one: set some order, laid out a year ahead in works— books, magazine, workshop, readings, film. Modest plans most, but a solid start for more ambitious work. Also setting up a small press collection in the public library. This first year one to grow on.

New book of Michael's poems, *Just Let Me Do It*, not bad. Some very fine poems inside covering much time from my Baltimore exit to now, poems I hadn't seen. Some hopelessly public in the way that when winning he is the best, but not all win. Michalea likes this one more than *Catch My Breath* or any other Lally she has seen. Ought to send mine to Gerald. Gerald sent three of my poems which are large, but not too big. Temporarily, they are somewhere in the house. Very handsome. Curious my feeling for my work. I said in a letter to him, distance not the best word. But it is long between and my feeling. There not being room for credit on that sheet, fitting. I look at them and imagine someone else having written. Just my knowing. Just my knowing.

8-20-78

Michalea away for four days to the country with Mary and baby in Missouri. It is her vacation in part, to get away. Very tempting for me but this becoming a record month of shop work. Work every weekend and some nights. I have misplaced copies of the poems Gerald set for me. Very handsome in the larger point size; set "As Passing," star poem, and the one of the cat playing with the bird's head. A real mystery as to where the stack of copies has gone, but in the house. Vanished and with them the original. I have only a single copy at work on the wall. —Try to bind copies of Michael's book tomorrow night. As many as I can.

10-5-78

The end of summer in the time past since last entry. Michalea returned from Missouri, and we spent the next two weeks working in the house. She did the bathroom and I did the dining room including refinishing the floor. Hard work; passable results. Julie Siegel and Peter Syvertsen visited for a few days. Rode with me back from Chicago Sept. 19th. Nice people. Busy times and the feeling on my part was that I longed for more time to spend with them, but a good visit. —So busy with the shop. Randy sick for a time making my load heavier there through August and September; both considerable work months. The pace has slowed somewhat now. Later this morning a reporter and camera crew will visit the shop for a one-shot feature story; this prompted by a news release we sent out on the reviews the books have been getting. Spent much of the day yesterday clearing and putting things in order. We also have set a date for the workshop we are doing for the Illinois Arts Council: November 10–11. As we can not afford to advertise the shop, this feature ought to help. At least it puts us in a good light; nine years of *Salt Lick* and books will be focused on Gem City.

10-28-78

Just awake not thinking.

The end of another month, suddenly for the journal. Days into weeks for the house and new winter. The shop. Books. We have had heat in the house for two days now, received our coal—14 tons. Most of a week spent on insulation of the attics with Dan. Hauled junk to the landfill, cleaned out the furnace myself this time and fired it. Some cutting and tacking of roll insulation left and that finished for this year. All things attendant to such work taking the days and evenings.—

Slow response so far for the workshop. Only one application and I worry that people won't respond thinking it all too quick to be managed. Still have to see.

The books have done as much as they can. I have filled most all orders. On the big one to Wilk, the Trammells are ready and the *Catch My Breath* by the end of the day tomorrow. Must. And I will feel so good to have it out. Response continues to be greater than any experienced. New orders weekly, slowing from the daily rate just after the first reviews. New review by Winch in D.C. and a possible review in *American Poetry Review* in Philadelphia. So, the press alive.

As soon as financial books are complete, hopefully by the end of the month of November, I will begin to think about the three new Lucky Hearts and magazine. There is a sort of careless attention for them until then in favor of everything else at hand.

Time for breakfast and then work. Happy most all. Love her quietly at times, tired with the day. Want to make the winter better for her.

11-12-78

Wrung out after the workshop. Two days on my feet, but proud of them. The way people came into the shop, listened, and then did is what I consider. Set type, printed cards with lines from Whitman's *Leaves* which I think is fitting. We also delivered a two hour history of printing which was surprisingly complete; most likely cut that to an hour if we do this again next year as it was just too much information for them. Our offset project which was a small pamphlet did not turn out as nicely as I had hoped, but passable. Many of the items chosen to illustrate are not square, therefore not square to the page, etc. And not having it done before had me rushing to complete. The students saw it happen though which is the important thing. They got right in there making their own stationery on the proof press, picked cuts and set type, then ran it. Only one misfortune which was Linda Williams appearing from Chicago. I should have been able to tell by the phone calls she made prior to the visit that she was not suited for the workshop, etc. Worst thing was her taking advantage of my efforts to settle her, thus making me her driver, clerk, hand-servant. Difficult to draw the lines that were finally demanded out of concern for the rest of the students. There was much support from Randy and Michalea and indeed, the rest of the workshop to have her fend for herself the way the rest of us were. David Pichaske from Peoria, who in a way was the best student, went more than halfway to help out w/ Linda, taking some of the load off me. In spite of her, a good experience in total.

Now. Making biscuits for breakfast. Will work this Sunday to clear the shop for jobs today. Breathe deep. Move things on. Think of poems.

11-15-78

worried with her heart
a small pain a
flutter she said here
and touched her breast

asleep now

she wanted me
to lay down to
her side   touch
her heart

for Steve Luecking

I thought of
a small animal slip
cast in plaster
that I had painted
held central
in a cube visible
that only worked
when you were there
everyones surprise

John Travis Watson

An external machinery of the heart. Your
teaching me as the girls oiled the early ones with
dipped feathers. *Treat everyone right. I always
did from the first one.*

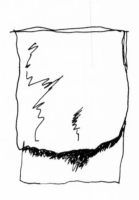

John T. Watson

Res: Park Plaza Nursing Home, Whitney
Born: April 18, 1885 in Robertson County, Texas
Died: November 29, 1978 at Whitney
Age: 93 years, 7 months and 11 days

History: Son of Mr. and Mrs. John T. Watson—
               lived near Franklin, Texas most of
               his life. Lived in Dallas for almost
               25 years. Moved to Whitney about
               three years ago. Married Floy Williams
               67 years ago.

Survivors: His wife, Floy Watson

               3 sons:
               A. W. Watson of Arlington
               L. C. Watson of College Station
               T. H. Watson of Austin

               4 daughters:
               Lois Gibbs of Houston
               Gladine Simon of Whitney
               Lucile Treadaway of Dallas
               Earline Davis of Garland

               14 grandchildren

               11 great grandchildren

12-18-78

Texas just about behind me. Grandaddy in the dirt there. This year just about gone. I'm slowly moving into the holidays. The thing that broke it for me being the giant Christmas tree we found discarded at the college. It had been in the cafeteria, but was put out when school closed. Michalea found it ("Jim, a seven foot tree.") and owing to our nearly penniless state we went for it. First in a car, then went for a truck. Once home, we placed it in the only spot it would go, the bay window. Twelve feet tall, six feet across, some nineteen feet circumference, perfect fit. A few presents under it. Will send pictures to Texas. —The travel and the rest has put me far behind in nearly all works.

12-28-78

The time between Christmas and New Year. Happy for Michalea. Busy at the shop. Time to get caught up with the books, the mail, the press. Reading. I finished *Jude the Obscure* and we think of a french one next. These last days are as if uncounted, off the records. I try to do my work and think of collection for the new year, self. Place to order. Pick up the letters.

Poems in Bodien's *New Journal.* Old illustration in the Spanish *Black on White* collection.

12-29-78

Sat with the cat and ate pecans and an orange this evening. Michalea visiting friends. Bill and Carrie in Michigan, so sat alone with the house. Sat with the cat. . . . End of the year, and we both inventory what has been done and that not. So that we know at once and then less so. A large feeling of things pending. New *Salt Lick* and new books. Have to sit with this journal soon and read through for the book. GB suggested my marking in the margin, then giving to him. Maybe, but have to try it.

mothers quilt gift
pretty top

think the hand
and manner all
ones

In any way, new year. I want to feel good with the journal. Need to have strength. Get on.

1-3-79

8 to 10 below zero again tonight. 8 inches of snow on
the ground. Real winter. Find myself day dreaming just a
little of spring's garden. Perhaps think more of a squash
book.

Sent copies of Toby Olson's review of *Catch My Breath*
to Michael and Gerald tonight. Getting the desk clear. Surprise today, second magazine in a month to arrive with my
work included. My "Wind Event" for Mieko Shiomi from
'74. Strange to have such a flurry of activity. Been a while.

1-6-79

After a letter from Gerald which spoke of his finishing
Specimen Days, I had Michalea get one for me from the
library. After reading *Jude,* I steadily tried to keep a level of
daily reading that is higher than I have managed through the
last year. But with the books, articles, ms. etc., there is always an hour or so before sleep. Read another 130 pages of
Michalea's novel, up to 382. Almost like getting into shape
again. And necessary for *A Quincy History.* Have just about
finished the selection for Michalea's book. Maybe finish this
weekend.

1-19-79

A squash book. Love poems. Talk about the food.

Squash flower the easier found morel. Not to dazzle beauty. Squash, tomatoes and okra plants enough to wear long sleeves in July. But to see water as rain or hose sprinkle just hit the dusty leaves and hear. Almost soft muffled hooves. In this new year. Zucchini and crooknecks.

The Boy Mistakes

street light out
of the window
not the moon
no   mistake

white blue the
new life

The new lights by glass pane surely moons after we are told. A love once described is in everything. Her hair by now the same. The open sky color is seen elsewhere. The beautiful beetles wings like your shirt.

2-21-79

Abed. Quietly. Michalea out to something. Early to bed at 10:00. Worked this evening and all this week on finishing more of Michael's book for orders and sending. Life with the shop is smoothing. We are doing more work in less time, equipment performing reasonably. I have tried since last week to move forward with the press and books. Sunday I cleared much of the business of desk, and now *Catch My Breath*. Will fill all existing orders by this weekend. Then begin to look seriously at the new books. Plan a meeting with Elaine, Michalea and Randy to settle that book. Talk to Gerald and finalize his. Sit with this journal and reread with eyes for a book . . . two of Julie's mss. to read and return. Her reading here very good. Michalea's reading also very fine. After flat ones, good ones so high.

3-2-79

Nearly sleep. Long days into quick weeks. Now March. Meet tomorrow with Elaine to plan Michalea's book. Gerald's *Spells* here in a few days. I hope to sit with this very soon. Will set a table of work to do and once done will select journal.

Two hours of reading for the magazine tonight. More poems from Julie, Jim Hubert, Alan Atkinson, Sheila Murphy, and Paul Shuttleworth sending. Toby Olson also a ms. Getting closer. Will talk to Dan again about a portfolio if he is interested.

3-14-79

Home for myself. Michalea in Chicago, 5:50 a.m. train, working on the phone for the college. Spending Friday with Judy. The house quietly for me. So working hard toward the backlog at the shop, and want to detail some duties here. Started reading journal tonight with editing in mind, but was disappointed starting at the front. Perhaps try another tack—maybe choose poems first, then see what fits well. Or go backwards. Would like to have the initial selection by her return. Not that I have waited for her leaving to do this. Just that when she is here I can not help listening and thinking to her. Listen for her.

> always want to be
> alive for what I hear
> from early
> the baby brothers teeth
> and went to the cabinet
> when told so in the kitchen
> where is the glass

*

backyard
figured hell directly
under the rock too
hard to dig out

3-20-79

Saw Ridge today. His first return visit after moving. Good feeling to talk with him, tell him how it happens, show him the shop. He looked good and is happy with his move. Thinks of finding employment of some sort. Also expects to be back in town in June.

Found out today that E. J. Retzinger has cancer, apparently in the liver and uncurable. He called Michalea and asked her if she would talk to him some about writing poetry. Noticed him attending the visiting poets readings, and I believe he has not missed any. He says he is accepting the fate. Wants to write some. I will try to visit him tomorrow.

4-12-79

Typing up the journal now. Much harder, but figure to type it all, then edit. Earliest pages finally vacant, save for the few spare moments of honesty. Otherwise, whistling past the headstones and enduring not so well being unknown. But knowing there is worth in upcoming pages makes the typing move ahead. Letter from GB to cheer me to the task. I can only see a brotherhood to *Specimen Days* in spirit of the daily. His being in the war changes it at first. If I could only. Pleasant window.

5-9-79

The days I spend walking in the country revive me. Several days last week I hunted mushrooms with Randy & Bill. Best year we've all had. We found both gray and yellow morels, mule tails, and two red types. One of the red ones called rosetops by the neighbors; the other red one known as "Elephant ears" as they appear more flesh-tone and constructed much as an ear with folds. We ate some tonight again.

In ways rested after the long and tiring walks. Printed Gerald's *A Book of Spells (first third)* which is as it was. The copy from Gerald was weak in cases, and all was askew due to misfeed of photocomposition printer. Developed with the paper misthreaded. My printing only fair. In its way, the book is complete. He knows it is coming, but no word yet. All printed up to the final run held up by CIP and © information/listing; collated to that point as well. Looks to be the first book I will have done completely before distribution was begun. Randy getting geared up to Michalea's. Paper here. Another batch of type ordered (better). And having my journal typed by the end of the month is my goal. Have not touched it in two weeks and let the mail pile up. I was in a period of inability. Slept too long, quiet weariness. I seem to be headed out of it.

5-10-79

The extent of our not knowing, as another life. Where the heat stops softly. Another one while the pace of the worlds passages.

5-23-79

> times the cows
> and sheep come home
>
> her waiting
>
> here
> I'll bring a child
> would you do

There behind the sheep. I hear wood being played above me, surely Bill.

Photo — Ivo Kamps

APPENDIX

Some Poems Mentioned
in the Text

RAMBLIN ROSE *Cycle*   {7 poems}

NOT VERY BOSTON BLACKY

being the first at the theater we
walked down the aisle openly
talking empty seats and curtain
drawn it was then that i noticed the feet
that is the shoes behind the curtain
we took a seat in the center

POEM FOR EMILY

If I read my poems to you
Around this oblique critic,
Don't wonder that I don't
Send bread, some flowers, a
Few flowers. I would bring
Them as their own messenger.
In your garden I would hide
Just to see you in your whiteness.
Your strength is where you walk.
I wait at my distances.

MY BROTHERS HAVE TAKEN THE CARTOONS TO TEXAS

and I have no television.
On Saturday morning,
there is no dull laughter
coming through the door:
no Rice-Chex in the rug.

THE TEST

yr usual face
its trying to read
yr finger prints
on my car door kitchen door
arm

like i told you once before
i would know the answers
if i saw them

POEM: A PHYSICS

to look at the chair
is to change it
the mystery
of the oak hardness
the shadow on the floor
a point in the galaxy

if the chair stood still
and the sun moved

THE GUEST

They have gone
to Osage Beach
for a short vacation
leaving their house to me.

It is Monday;
during the day I write
and feed their dog
and sometimes

the phone rings:
I tell them
no one is home
for days.

MESSAGE TO THE CHIEF

i dreamed a dream about the bats
that come from carlsbad caverns
about the cowboys and what it
must of felt like seeing them
come and leave again so many
blackbrown cloud rising slowly
mammal

SOUTHWEST

I know the taste
of grease from a cheap
cafe on my way through
Oklahoma; 4 in the morning.
I had missed Atoka, but
it had stopped raining.

I had cousins in McAlister

before I left years ago,
before I left my grandmother
                in Dallas,
before I left my wife,
even before we were married,

she was a waitress.

POEM FOR FATHER GOING
CROSSCOUNTRY

It's been almost a year
since I've seen the family.

Outside the cafe
by your truck loaded
with jet engines
going to Omaha and then
to Tinker Field just this side
of Oklahoma City, you tell me
about the time you carried
eight helicopter
engines all stood on end
from Conn. to Dover, Delaware.
And how you worried about going
through an underpass that was
too low, knocking all the engines down.
You remembered driving past
a hold, 35 x 50 feet, thinking
it was just road repairs and then
reading in the papers about the
dynamite truck exploding
from a sniper's bullet: there was nothing
found of the driver.

Of course, I don't stay up here to
hurt you or Momma or make you
feel bad. You know that.
It's Triavil now for three weeks
just to see what happens.

Drive carefully. Watch the roads.
Your truck.
Yes, I'll be there this Christmas.

A LEGEND OF FAMOUS MEN

—for Bob & Ginger

i.
the men
have come
the ruptured
artery
has caused
these old
buildings
discomfort

ii.
the long
weakening
wall suddenly
burst
sewage loose
the cool
sand that
had packed
against
the pipe
quickly eaten
away

iii.
this street
cancer the
men digging
above

STARTING BACK TOWARD THE CABIN

still thinking of you.
The sun finally gone behind
the pasture.
Soon the trees will
be darker against the sky.

Have you ever in a field
been dark alone?
Do you know about fences
that become invisible at night
and wait to rip at arms, legs,
maybe a throat, horses & deer,
men.

I strip a short branch
and whip at the weeds as if
I could still see them.

ORANGE POEM

a child is crying
while his mother
eats oranges
the child has fallen

from the earth
floating among the orange peels
scared of oranges
peels and juices

a child is eating oranges
while his mother sits
on the porch in the glider
like a tourist
quietly watching trees

EVERYONE'S RIVER POEM

The Mississippi has backed up
into all the sloughs and finger
creeks that reach deeply to the
highway.

As I drive through this bottom road
afternoon I imagine my car suddenly turning
off the pavement, over the edge of the road
bounding, lurching, and tilting down
the soft bank. All the scrub underbrush
scratching at the doors and windows
like witches.

& then control and return
back to the road, stretching
water in the distance.

Beside me on the seat is nothing.

I wonder how many cars have gone under
water   drivers beating at the windows
with their fists and heels.

EXERCISE

two perfect vertical lines can
cause the arm
to collapse the color of the shirt
seeming to flood over the arm
seen just before disappearing

the side of the head as
if hit with a board the
bones under crushed
sliding

if yr face is too round
people will think of tires
roundness in objects the warmth
slowly dissipating

if too square you could be a hitler
or eva braun or roosevelt i
couldnt trust you

make yr figure slightly irregular
make the features undistinguished you
know about the face
make the year early 50s say
1950

RANDY TELLS ME ABOUT HIS GREAT UNCLE SCHUYLER

He bought a huge jar
of peanut butter
and got sick after
eating it all. He
couldn't eat peanut
butter again.

A mouse crawled
in his mouth while
he was sleeping.
He bit it in half
and found part of it
when he woke up.

During a dust storm
in Kansas, he hid
in an abandoned
locomotive boiler
and died because
he couldn't get out.

GRANDFATHER

you taught me:

Roofing from 5:30 to 9 in the morning
and then 4:30 till we couldn't see to hammer
straight. Because of the heat, my first real sunburn.

How I could mark the Bible (King James edition)
with bobby pins and red pencils for easy
recollection of verses.

Practice; a pad and pencil and several five
figure columns to sum. You checked them; we
did this after supper.

How my uncle Alfred who had taught at West Point
could have married a beautiful German girl from
Fort Worth till he sneaked in her bed one night.

Hammering, nailing, sawing, post-hole digging,
and most important pride so I could build
anything I ever wanted. You mentioned a chicken coop.

To watch wrestling on Saturday nights. A mask
on a contender meant he had something to hide.

How women wearing pants and smoking were predictions
come true: a passage in Revelations. More red lines
and more talk about the Ethiopians.

To read the papers, listen to Paul Harvey, think
of every man as good until he does something.

GRANDMOTHER

you taught me:

How bacon doesn't need grease since it makes its own,
too much shortening makes the biscuits fall apart,
you don't have to have meat every meal.

Sewing, cutting out patterns for quilts, crocheting.
No knitting because it is too warm for much wool in Dallas.
Aprons made of the same cloth as the quilts, potholders, divan
    pillows.

To do what I wanted to do because you thought I would make it.
Our people in Oklahoma think I will be just like my Daddy.
Sonny's divorced and racing and wrecking cars while Arthur Ray
brought a wife back from Turkey.

To watch out for my brothers when we get teamed up on,
to run till we could find a stick, to see that tv wrestling
as all a big show. No truth in it.

To save things: foil, detergent bottles, and tiles.
You can always use them to hold some little something.
She catches rainwater for her elephant ears.

PRAYER

we eat tomatoes
bread

and drink milk

and they are sweet

THE CIRCLE *Cycle*   {15 poems}

LOVELETTER

after the letter i
write my letter

don't worry
who knows who will be famous
the trip was long and i am
tired   you're right about most
of it   i do what i can and
that is too much   i suppose
this letter was written years ago
and i'm just now mailing it

DAUGHTER

father after the wake
greets the guests and
asks them to sign the
register

father after the service
leads the immediate family
to the hearse he brings his hand
to mothers black shoulders

father after the short
layoff from work starts
writing me again
with no return address on
his envelopes that way

he knows i get them

SITUATION POETIC

the moths are everywhere
now that it is summer

it was never this bad before
they get in the ice box
when i open the door they're
in the can with the grease
the glasses with water the pans
waiting for wash they ram the
bulb overhead and get tangled in
my hair

        it's too late tonight
to worry about it i'll turn off
the light and hunt them in the
morning dead among the dishes

TO SEE THE CHILDREN

just off the bus
here in another river
town

in one block
mays drugs
awerkamp machine co.
and the car wash stalls

his suit case is black
and tin and he lives close
enough to walk to the house

ALONG THE RIVERROAD

wild lilies and indian coral
trim the highway

the road recently redone
dark and smooth in patches

three trees in the fence row
topped and then felled fence high

the fence against the tree
part of it

its bark that holds the fence
upright the staples

covered by the trees growing
the wire deeper in the tree

each year

CONVERSATION

sweeping
out the house

hair cat hair
ashes bugs marijuana
paper crumbs

we   all live in this
house   these are ours

AFTER THE CHORUS

of the drinking song
by the father,
William was asked
to recite some. A
little Browning some
one said.

He wheeled on the stool
from the piano, stood
upright, rode his vest
down, and eyeing the ceiling
light began.

* * * * * * * * * *

It was Paul that sold the
painting and went to London
after his mother died. She
kept him from the pits:
black lung, the sudden rumble
across the village which
meant bodies.

* * * * * * * * * *

Arthur died in the mine.
Only the day before he
had won two shillings
by diving off a bridge.
The scrape from the tin
cans caused his leg to swell,
but he was taking his mother
to the fair.

* * * * * * * * * *

After the love for husband
failed, she loved her sons.
Paul she loved too much: she

owned him. Her weak heart
suddenly turning a last time
left him free.

* * * * * * * * * *

Father came home with black
face and stiff clothes.

PECANS

Living in Lancaster,
the neighboring
family would let
me go with them
for pecans.

The father who sold
eggs to the Veterans
Hospital would go
with us, his wife & boys,
the first day to shake
the trees down.

2½ days or 3
would clean the
small grove
trees lining
a ridge over
the limestone wash
just south of the coops.

The pecans under the leaves:
stones to the feet.

JOHNDADDY

we had been hoeing
peas or cotton i
dont know which but
i had been burdened
down all day

daddy called me in
and on the way
to the house i
began to tremble
threw down my hoe
and grabbed the branch
of a peach tree that
was there crying
crying gave myself
to the Lord

i went in
the house
a gentleman
and been
one since

THE MAILMAN'S DILEMMA

each mornings coffee leaves its ring
on the filing cabinet

TEXT

from Lawrence

1. TEMPERANCE

Driving too fast could be dangerous. The car leaving
the road at a high rate of speed could keep you from
eating again. Too much of one thing.

2. SILENCE

The window open for breeze if there is one.

3. ORDER

To what you say, it shows you where
the voice comes from, how loudly
it can move, where it lives,
where to align the person in the town.

4. RESOLUTION

The ulcer as houseguest must leave. The empty guest bed helps
the host sleep at night.

5. FRUGALITY

Demand nothing of others. Give what is needed. Be a rose.

6. INDUSTRY

The difference between what you think and where you
live is how you build the house.

7. SINCERITY

Don't ask friends to hang pictures. A nail in another
hand is not your nail. And the hammer.

8. JUSTICE

"The only justice is to follow the sincere intuition of
the soul, angry or gentle. Anger is just, and pity is
just, but judgment is never just."

9. MODERATION

Of the best of   . Absolutes are weaknesses. You
are closing too early.

10. CLEANLINESS

Man being unpure is polluted by too many purities. The
best looking is usually stolen.

11. TRANQUILITY

Short divorcing of the village. The music of
earth history can not be heard by the musicians
except in the dressing rooms. Respect your silences.

12. CHASTITY

Give honestly.

13. HUMILITY

Each a different species. Taking is spiritual, and
while giving, listen.

BEHEMOTH

the horizon

road rises
to cross the
tracks

the giant
looming
with our
billboards
at his feet

to comprehend
him

SIRENS

sitting on the roof
of the building
our feet to other feet
each in the circle

sirens
momentarily in the city
sirens

POEM

four hunters
in the valley
of the buffalo herd

one hunter is killed
one buffalo is killed

women and their small children
and the hunters all eat
the buffalo under trees

THE CIRCLE

the circus
as we all know
here in the
country

comes to town
when it is close
enough to go see

we travel the blacktop
past the radio towers
to the five points
several to a car
and the ride is routine

getting back is always
late near the sun

the circle

UNCOLLECTED

NEW KITTENS

three
on the pile of
clean tee shirts
next to the bed
jaffee the mother
had gone in
last night when i hadnt
seen her

THE NIGHT WE HAD OUR LOGIC LESSON

the risk game was disrupted
because he thought i was cheating
he quit the game

we argued about logic all night
screaming about eating things that
are the wrong color

we ate breakfast when the sun

SIR

The new cadets not knowing
the right from left foot
had to see their feet as hay
or straw to know the difference,
where to turn while marching,
the pillbox, that man:
so you gave them a song
to sing.

The mother washing her
children's feet knows that
it keeps the sheets clean
in the summer besides helping
them get to sleep in so
much heat.

THE WRENCH

that turns
the bolt

is a club
another tool
the way we
live here

with our tools
not all tools

KITCHEN TALKING

There is always a place
to pray. The woman
in the afternoon in the
kitchen finds herself
only with the supper
and pantry.
　　　　　Sitting with stove
and door to her back
she puts the dish towel
over her head. When she
is here, she talks to heaven.